A Candlelight Ecstasy Romance ®

"ARE YOU GOING TO MAKE ME PAY FOR ANOTHER MAN'S MISTAKES?" STEVE ASKED FURIOUSLY, CLENCHING THE WHEEL IN HIS FISTS. "THAT'S NOT FAIR!"

"If you want to talk about fair, I'm not the one who changed the rules," Barbara answered, hitting the seat with her palm.

"Yes, damn it, I changed the rules! I thought you loved me!"

"Of course, I love you!" she cried. "Do you think I'd put a man whom I loved through being married to me? It's because I love you that I'm saying no."

"That's ridiculous!" Steve flared. "Think about this weekend and what we shared, and then tell me you won't marry me. I'll bet you can't do it."

"No!" Barbara protested, sitting up in the seat. "Yes, yes, I can say no. Oh, Steve, don't you understand? I can be your lover, but not your wife."

A CANDLELIGHT ECSTASY ROMANCE ®

DELICATE BALANCE

Emily Elliott

A CANDLELIGHT ECSTASY ROMANCE ®

Published by
Dell Publishing Co., Inc.
1 Dag Hammarskjold Plaza
New York, New York 10017

Dell ® TM 681510, Dell Publishing Co., Inc.

Candlelight Ecstasy Romance®, 1,203,540, is a registered
trademark of Dell Publishing Co., Inc.,
New York, New York.

ISBN: 0-440-11817-4

Printed in the United States of America
First printing—October 1983

To Our Readers:

We have been delighted with your enthusiastic response to Candlelight Ecstasy Romances®, and we thank you for the interest you have shown in this exciting series.

In the upcoming months we will continue to present the distinctive sensuous love stories you have come to expect only from Ecstasy. We look forward to bringing you many more books from your favorite authors and also the very finest work from new authors of contemporary romantic fiction.

As always, we are striving to present the unique, absorbing love stories that you enjoy most—books that are more than ordinary romance.

Your suggestions and comments are always welcome. Please write to us at the address below.

Sincerely,

The Editors
Candlelight Romances
1 Dag Hammarskjold Plaza
New York, New York 10017

CHAPTER ONE

If anyone had told Barbara Weimer on that hot September morning that her life was about to be turned upside down, she would have laughed out loud. Barbara Weimer was firmly in control of her life and her emotions, and no one and nothing was going to change that.

Humming softly, Barbara entered the small office building in Houston where she had been in private family practice for two years and smiled at her pretty young receptionist. Sylvia Vasquez smiled back and blew unselfconsciously on her wet fingernails, painted in a shade of vivid purple. "Good morning, Dr. Weimer," she called breezily. "We've got an office full already. You're late."

"I got held up at the hospital," Barbara explained as she slipped a white coat over her red slacks and white shirt and pulled back her waist-length silver-blond hair into a loose ponytail. Absently she noticed that a button was missing on her cuff but she had too much to do to worry about it. "That cute little Martinez baby fell and split his lip open, and I stitched him up in the emergency room while I was down there rather than have them come here. So how many of them out there are for me?" she asked as she peeked out into the packed office. She recognized some as her patients and others as her partner Max's, but about half were unfamiliar to her.

"A lot of them are yours," Sylvia said as she carefully picked up the telephone receiver so as not to smudge her wet nails. She entered another name into the appointment book while Barbara checked the telephone messages littering her desk. None were emergencies, so she put them aside to be dealt with later and headed toward the first examining room to see her first patient of the day.

Sally Peters balanced her eight-month-old daughter on her hip and tried in vain to distract the fussy baby. Barbara picked up the squirming baby and tickled her gently, delighting in the way the sturdy little girl wiggled in her arms and cooed wetly all over her white coat. Gently but deftly she laid Wendy down and coaxed the tiny mouth open with a tongue depressor, and from what she saw she diagnosed a simple sore throat. She took a throat culture and prescribed baby aspirin until she could be sure from the culture that the infection was bacterial. Casually she asked Sally how her husband's diet was coming, and was delighted to learn that Tom Peters had lost ten pounds and was determined to lose more. Barbara snitched a sloppy kiss from Wendy and bade Sally good-bye.

In the next room Marilyn Harris, the college-aged daughter of one of her patient families, was seated nervously on the examining table. Barbara smiled warmly at the girl, her bright blue eyes crinkling at the corners. "What seems to be the problem?" she asked routinely.

Marilyn blushed a fiery shade of red. "I'm not sick or anything," she said uncertainly. "It's just that my boyfriend and I—we're in love and all. . . ." Finally Marilyn blurted, "I need some birth control!"

"Well, that's reasonable," Barbara said calmly as she stifled a smile of amusement at Marilyn's embarrassment. "Is he a nice young man?" she asked softly.

"Oh, yes," Marilyn replied with enthusiasm, her embarrassment fading. "We've been going together for the last six months."

"It sounds as if you know him pretty well," Barbara replied, relieved that Marilyn at least had known the boy for a while. "As far as the birth control goes, there are a number of reliable methods to choose from, although at your age and with your need for complete protection, I recommend the pill."

8

Marilyn nodded, then looked at Barbara curiously. "You won't say anything to the folks about this, will you?"

"Of course not," Barbara replied, allowing herself to smile encouragingly at the girl. "You're of age and it isn't any of their business. Besides, I'd rather have you on the pill than in here pregnant in two months." Barbara hesitated and bit her lip.

Marilyn immediately picked up on Barbara's hesitation. "If you want to say something, Dr. Weimer, go ahead. I don't mind."

"Thanks," Barbara said, nodding her head. "Just one thing. Respect yourself and your body, okay? And be sure that he does, too."

Marilyn nodded. "Of course, Dr. Weimer," she said softly. "I'd never go off the deep end like some of my friends have."

"Good!" Barbara said, much relieved. "Now, my nurse will help you get undressed, and I'll be back shortly to give you an examination."

Marilyn smiled with genuine affection at Barbara. "Thanks, Dr. Weimer."

Barbara went out the door, humming softly. So Marilyn thought she was in love! Barbara's lips twitched a little as she picked up Jim Bailey's chart and flipped through it. Marilyn was really too young for that serious a relationship, Barbara thought as she pushed open the door of the next examining room, but thank goodness the girl did not just want to be promiscuous.

Barbara's next patient, Jim Bailey, was an older man with high blood pressure. She then treated three patients in a row for gastroenteritis. Next she gave a follow-up exam to a heart patient, and had to fuss rather severely at a middle-aged diabetic who insisted that just a little cake would not hurt her. Barbara showed each patient warm concern and treated them with professional skill. And she never quite stopped humming under her breath.

Barbara loved her work. She had chosen family practice as a specialty because she liked it so much. The work was hard, the

9

hours were long, and the pay was not quite as generous as that in some other specialties, but it allowed her to become involved on a personal level with her patients, and that involvement was what she wanted. She enjoyed knowing her patients, each one interesting her as both a case and a person. She was still humming softly under her breath at noon when she finished with her last patient. She poured a hasty cup of coffee from the urn that Sylvia kept warm in the small kitchen and slipped out of her lab coat. As she sipped the hot brew, her eyes strayed out the window at the monolith that was being erected across the street. It was a huge concrete-and-glass affair, large and modern but still surprisingly graceful, boldly rising up to meet the big Texas sky.

"I wonder who designed that monstrosity," Max grumbled as he poured himself a cup of coffee and shed his white coat. Barbara had seen Max to nod to him as they whisked in and out of their examining rooms, but this was the first chance they had had really to speak. Max was not his usual smiling self, and Barbara turned exasperated eyes on him. He was a few years older than her thirty-two, but today he looked worn and tired.

"Did Marcie keep you out late again?" Barbara asked shrewdly. Marcie was Max's current girl friend and hoped to be Mrs. Vaughan number two.

Max nodded ruefully. "I disappointed her last week when I had that delivery on her birthday, and I promised her that I would make it up to her. One of her friends was giving a party, and she really wanted to go."

"Didn't you bother to tell her that you had been up most of the night before with Mrs. Caswell's heart attack?" Barbara sighed.

"I know, I know," Max admitted. "I should have said so. But sometimes I just can't say no to her." Max looked at Barbara, asking her with his expression to understand.

Barbara understood only too well. Max was one of the most unassertive people she had ever met. He couldn't say no to anyone. Caught between his greedy ex-wife, his demanding and

10

jealous girl friend, and his whining mother, Max was wearing himself out trying to please all of them and succeeding with none. Barbara was becoming seriously concerned about him and did not hesitate to say so.

"Damn it, Max, if you don't slow down and take a little time and money for yourself, I'm going to be treating you for a heart attack, and then I'll have both your and my patients to treat. The next time Eileen comes in here with her hand out, just say you're all out this week, and for God's sake, tell Marcie to entertain herself every so often." Barbara grimaced as Max's face fell. "I didn't mean that like it sounded," she said softly. "I'm just worried about you, that's all."

Max nodded. "I know that," he said, "and I'll try." But Barbara was unconvinced, and she shook her head with concern. Straightening her shoulders, she turned to the window and eyed the structure that Max had criticized.

"I don't think it's so bad," she said as she stared at the half-finished building and chewed her lower lip.

"You don't think what's so bad?" Max asked. "Oh, that," he said as she gestured toward the window. He ran his hand through his curling dark hair and grinned impishly. "It isn't. I just felt like grousing. Want to go to the local greasy spoon for a bite?"

"Thanks, but I want to check on Lorena Valdez before this afternoon's horde descend upon me. Thanks, though," Barbara said as she watched Max's retreating form. She shook her hair free and secured it with combs, a faintly disturbed expression on her graceful oval face as she left the building. Tall, lithe, handsome, Max made most women's hearts beat a little faster and many of his female patients had crushes on him, but Barbara's feelings for him were strictly platonic. Which was a good thing, she thought as she climbed into her blue Corvette and pitched a medical journal over the seat, where it landed on top of another journal and a stethoscope. An office romance was the surest way in the world to destroy a partnership, she thought as she roared out of the parking lot, and both of them valued their working relationship too much to jeopardize it in that way. Still, Barbara was becoming more and more baffled by her response, or, more accurately, her lack of response, to the many attractive men with whom she came in contact. Was something wrong with her these days? Max had his share of sex appeal, as did many of the other doctors, but she simply could not respond to them as men anymore, and frankly this scared her. Had she become cold? She rubbed her knuckles across her forehead as she waited impatiently for the light to change. Damn Wayne, had he done this to her? Had living with him for so long and then going through that bitter divorce made her lose her ability to feel anything for a man anymore? Had all the pain and the bitterness changed her from a loving woman into an iceberg?

Barbara parked her car in one of the sacred parking spaces allotted to doctors and strode into Memorial Hospital. Her thoughts had returned to Mrs. Valdez and she was unaware of the young orderly and the middle-aged doctor who stopped what they were doing to watch the beautiful woman stride confidently down the wide corridors of the large private hospital and into ICU. She was tall and slender, although her breasts were round and full and her hips were womanly. Her hair, released from the casual working ponytail, tumbled almost to her waist and shimmered like silk even under the artificial lights in the corridor. A frown of concentration pulled her soft sensuous lips out of line. The beginnings of laugh lines around her bright blue eyes and permanent dark circles under them, legacies of the strenuous years spent in training, gave her age away, but very few of her many masculine admirers were complaining. In fact, there had been frank enthusiasm from some of the unattached doctors when she had finally terminated her unhappy marriage, but so far Barbara had avoided dating any of them and their glee was turning into puzzlement.

Barbara pushed open the swinging doors into ICU and edged her way into the crowded nurses' station. She retrieved Mrs.

Valdez's chart from one of her favorite nurses and gently teased the girl about her increasingly apparent pregnancy. The nurses reported that Mrs. Valdez had been difficult to handle and had repeatedly demanded to be taken home. Barbara sympathized with the nurses, glad that it was usually they who had to deal with the old folks who wanted to go home so badly. Barbara was not to get off the hook today, however; Mrs. Valdez subjected her to the same tirade she had inflicted on the nurses. Barbara promised her that they would release her just as soon as they could, but she shook her head as she closed the door on Mrs. Valdez. She did not like the look of the electrocardiograms that had been taken that morning. Mrs. Valdez's heart was very old and weak, and it was unlikely that she would ever get to go home. Heavyhearted, Barbara walked back to the nurses' station slowly. She sincerely liked the tart-tongued little lady, and was grieved that her long life was almost over.

Barbara spent fifteen minutes talking with Mrs. Valdez's son and daughter-in-law, explaining to them as gently as she could that Mrs. Valdez was very close to death and that she and the nurses would do everything they could to make the last few days as painless for Mrs. Valdez as possible. Mr. Valdez reminded Barbara of his mother's wish that Barbara be there when the end came, and Barbara made a note on the chart that she was to be called when that time was near. Gasping at the time, she hurried out of the hospital and drove back to her office as quickly as she could. She ran in the back door of the office, platinum hair flying in the wind, unaware of a pair of intent hazel eyes watching her from a scaffold high above the ground.

Again greeted by a full waiting room, Barbara grabbed a hasty cup of coffee and began another round of patients. In some ways it was a repetition of her morning's work, but several patients had called at the last minute with legitimate reasons to see her, so even though her last patient was scheduled for four thirty, it was well after six when she finished. Wearily she walked back to the kitchen for yet another cup of coffee before making her afternoon telephone calls.

Sylvia poked her head around the corner. "The typing you wanted is on your desk. May I go on now? I have a date with the most macho male you ever laid eyes on!"

"I thought you had a date with him last week," Barbara said teasingly. Sylvia was a confirmed fan of the male sex, admiring the species and pursuing her quarry with a skill and dedication that would have put the average lion hunter to shame. In the six months she had worked for Barbara and Max, she had dated a foreign-car mechanic, a rookie policeman, two car salesmen, and a stripper at the local women's bar. The young girl's escapades were a never-ending source of amusement to Barbara and the rest of the staff, and Barbara was not above egging Sylvia on when she launched into one of her rapturous descriptions of her latest find. "So what's this one like?" Barbara asked wickedly. "He couldn't be any better than the one last week!"

"Oh, yes, he is!" Sylvia exclaimed. "He puts the last one to shame! He's tall, blond, has a mouth like—"

"Spare me the details," Max interrupted dryly. "Sylvia, hadn't you better go on?" Sylvia glided out the door, leaving Max staring exasperatedly at Barbara, who was by now laughing out loud. "Why do you deliberately get her started?" he asked.

Barbara stuck out her tongue at Max. "Why did you stop her?" She giggled. "It was just getting good!"

"Women!" Max shook his head as he headed for his office. Barbara vowed to wait patiently until morning for her description of this latest Adonis, knowing that, with a little prompting, Sylvia would give the entire staff a blow-by-blow account of her latest trophy.

Barbara carried her coffee cup back to her desk and picked up her list of names and numbers. She swallowed the last of the lukewarm coffee and grimaced at the bitter aftertaste. She had picked up the coffee habit during her residency, when one-hundred-twenty-hour workweeks demanded some sort of stimulant to keep her going. She picked up the telephone and dialed the first number. Some of the problems required an office visit, but many of them could be dealt with over the telephone. Barbara kicked off her shoes and settled back in her chair. Sinking gratefully into the padded cushions, she rubbed one aching foot against the other and sighed with relief. The chair felt good to her tired body.

Nearly an hour later she finished her last call and hung up the telephone. Max had stuck his head in the door and waved her good-bye a few minutes ago, and the usually bustling office was strangely silent. Barbara shed her white coat and rummaged in her desk drawer for her purse. Her footsteps echoed hollowly in the hall as she walked toward the back exit.

Barbara jumped at the sound of sharp knuckles rapping loudly on the front door. She was momentarily frightened, but realized that anyone who meant her harm would not be making that much noise. Quickly she changed direction and walked through the darkened waiting room. Pulling a large key-ring from her purse, she selected the proper key and unlocked the thick glass door. A dirty, disheveled construction worker stared at her in disappointment. "I was looking for the doctor," he said breathlessly. "Has he gone home for the day?"

"I'm an M.D.," Barbara said in a businesslike tone. "What seems to be the problem?"

The man looked at her in astonishment, then grinned. "I wonder if my old lady would let me come to you for my next physical?" he said with a leer. Barbara grinned at him and winked impudently. Sobering quickly, he continued. "There's been an accident on the site over there. A couple of men are hurt, and we can't reach either of their doctors. Can you come help?"

"Of course," Barbara responded quickly, her adrenaline flowing as it always did in an emergency.

She returned to her office and grabbed her medical bag, then followed the man across the busy thoroughfare, deftly darting through the heavy traffic. Once they were on the site, the man stopped at a trailer and handed her a hard hat. "It's dangerous where we're going," he explained solemnly. Barbara looked up at the half-finished monolith and swallowed a huge lump in her throat. There were numerous platforms at various heights, but the one that appeared to be inhabited was fifteen stories off the ground. Shaking a little, Barbara tucked her hair up under the hard hat and followed the man to an open outside elevator.

As they were about to step on, a burly middle-aged man ran from the trailer to the elevator, bellowing like an elephant, his pounding feet kicking up little clouds of dust. "I send you for a doctor, Jenkens, and you bring some damned young nurse! You expect to put her on the elevator? I told you to get a doctor!"

Jenkens opened his mouth to speak, but the older man continued. "Damn it, man, you think a broad in a ponytail can take care of the men up there? Now, get your stupid butt back to that office and come back with a doctor!"

He turned back to the trailer, but Barbara's angry words cut through the air like a knife. "I am a doctor, damn you, and I didn't come all this way to tangle with some middle-aged redneck who doesn't like my ponytail! Now, get the hell out of the way. There are men up there who need my help!" She elbowed her way past the foreman and got on the outdoor elevator.

The older man's face turned a mottled shade of purple. Without speaking another word, he climbed on the elevator with them and turned the control lever to UP. With a sickening lurch the elevator began a slow, jerking ascent up the side of the building. Feeling herself grow clammy, Barbara focused her eyes on a distant skyscraper and willed herself to remain calm. She had patients at the top of this climb, and she would be of little use to them if she was a bundle of nerves.

Finally the elevator came to a halt, although at this height it swayed in the wind. Jenkens alighted onto the wooden platform first and extended his hand to Barbara. She took it gratefully and gracefully leaped onto the platform, where a steel beam was hanging at a ragged angle across the walkway, and beyond the beam two men were lying unconscious in the middle of a group of onlookers. Jenkens crawled over the beam and nonchalantly grasped Barbara around the waist and lifted her over. The surly middle-aged man followed with her medical bag.

A quick visual inspection of the two men revealed that they were both healthy and somewhere in their thirties. One of them was wearing the typical dirty jeans and shirt of a construction worker, and one of his legs was twisted under him at an unnatural angle. The other had a nasty gash that was bleeding profusely. She noted idly that the one with the head injury was dressed casually but neatly in khaki slacks and an open shirt. Barbara quickly removed a gauze pad from her bag and pressed on the wound. When she had temporarily stopped the flow of blood, she motioned to the middle-aged man. Curiously, he hung back.

Barbara scowled at him. She needed his assistance. Couldn't he tell? "Come hold this tourniquet for me, Mr.—?" she snapped.

"Fisk," the man replied. Slowly he came forward, and taking a deep breath, gingerly he pressed the gauze into the wound. Blood started to flow freely again.

Barbara mashed down on Fisk's hand until the blood ceased flowing. "Now, hold it!" she ordered, exasperated. She turned to her other patient, who was beginning to regain consciousness and moan softly. "Mr. Jenkens, I need for you to ease him up just a little. His leg has a nasty break in it and I'm never going to get him down that damned elevator until I get it splinted." Jenkens pulled the man up, freezing when the victim let out with a bellow of pain. Barbara winced at the pitiful sound in spite of herself. "Easy, fella," she said soothingly as she withdrew an injection of Demerol from her bag. She plunged the needle into his arm and waited for a moment for the pain-killer to take effect.

Barbara motioned to the other onlooking workers. "I need a board, about three to six inches wide, and some wide cloth strips—lots of those. And something we can use as makeshift stretchers." The onlookers nodded, and several of them headed toward the elevator and disappeared down the side of the building. Barbara skillfully probed the rapidly swelling calf with firm yet gentle fingers. This break would need surgery, and she should probably call in an orthopedic surgeon to do it. The broken ends of the lower leg bones were a shattered, crumbling mass under her fingers. She looked at the man with genuine sympathy. Although his injuries were certainly not permanent, he had several weeks of real discomfort ahead as the shattered bones healed. Poor man! Barbara's heart went out to him. She sincerely hoped that the accident wouldn't keep him out of work for long and that he'd have a full recovery.

She turned back to her other patient. He was still unconscious, but showed only mild signs of shock. Still, Barbara hated a head injury accompanied by unconsciousness. The actual condition of the patient could not accurately be assessed until he regained consciousness, and the waiting was always an anxious time. Sincerely hoping for the best, she crawled over to him and lightly ran her fingers over his body, checking for any further injury and finding none. She noted with appreciation that he was in superb physical condition, with lean hard muscles that got a regular workout somewhere, and that his watch and shoes were in a price range well beyond a simple worker's income.

The crew returned with a flat board and some freshly torn strips of cloth, as well as two army surplus stretchers that smelled musty. Barbara turned back to the man with the broken leg and quickly positioned his leg on the board and bound it up as tightly as she dared; then, very carefully, two of the men lifted him onto the stretcher. Barbara returned to Fisk and pushed his hand away from the unconscious man's head wound, probing it gently as blood wet her hand and the cuff of her blouse. Fisk turned to the workers and mumbled something unintelligible.

"This man won't lose that much blood on the way to the hospital," she volunteered. "Have you called an ambulance?" Jenkens shook his head. "Well, don't, then," Barbara said crisply. "We'll put them in one of your vans, and I'll meet you at

Memorial. The man with the broken leg should go down first, and I'll ride with him. Fisk, put the tourniquet back on that one."

"But—"

"Do it," she ordered.

It was even more harrowing on the way down, with the wind gently blowing the elevator back and forth. Barbara forced herself to concentrate on the welfare of her patients and not think about the swaying contraption that she was riding in, but she still had broken out in a cold sweat by the time they were halfway down the side of the building. Finally they reached the ground and Barbara supervised the loading of her patient into the back of a luxurious air-conditioned van with SULLIVAN CONSTRUC-TION boldly emblazoned on the side. Barbara watched as the elevator made its second descent and two workers carried the second man to the van and carefully laid him inside. Barbara motioned to Fisk to get in the van, but the older man shook his head and lurched toward the trailer. Another young man climbed in the back of the van and positioned the tourniquet. Laughing, Jenkens hopped into the cab and switched on the ignition.

"What's with him?" Barbara asked, thumbing toward Fisk.

"He can't stand the sight of blood," Jenkens answered, laughing, as he roared out of the driveway.

Barbara hung up the telephone in the emergency room and turned to Jenkens. "I've called in an orthopedic surgeon to see the man with the broken leg. I need for you to notify the next of kin and give the nurse here some information about the injured men."

Jenkens motioned for the man who had ridden in the back of the van. "Joe, why don't you talk to the nurse about Al, since you two are good buddies." Joe followed the nurse and Jenkens turned to Barbara. I'll tell you what I can about Mr. Sullivan," he continued as he loped down the hall behind her. Barbara opened the door to a small trauma room and handed the information form to an aide who had come into the room behind them. She was pleased to note that the man had regained consciousness, although he was still dazed and in no condition to answer questions for the aide. Jenkens perched on a stool and proceeded to answer the aide's questions while Barbara tended to her patient. She tied back her hair and washed her hands thoroughly, then scrubbed the area of the wound, a deep triangular gash just above his left eyebrow. The man moaned softly at her ministrations but said nothing. As she recleaned her hands, she listened with half an ear to Jenkens describing her patient. Steve Sullivan. An address in a prestigious neighborhood off of Westheimer Road. Age thirty-five. Divorced. Owner of Sullivan Construction. Barbara stepped back and looked again at her patient, adding her own notes to Jenkens's monologue. Tall. Lean. Light-brown hair bleached by the sun. Simple fracture of the nose at some point in his life. Hazel eyes becoming more alert by the minute. Face that was too angular and lined and hard to be handsome, but probably more interesting that way, anyway. Definite overall masculine appeal. Bedroom eyes. Sensuous lower lip.

Bedroom eyes! Sensuous lower lip! What was she thinking? This man was a patient, not a movie star pinup to be swooned over as if she were some man-crazy adolescent! Tearing her thoughts away from her patient's attributes, she gave him a single shot of Novocaine near the wound and inserted the needle through the loose folds of skin, carefully drawing them together. Stimulated by the pain, the man moaned and tried to pull away. Cautiously Barbara put in a second stitch.

Steve Sullivan finally began to take notice of his surroundings, surveying her with dazed hazel eyes that were focusing for the first time on her intent blue ones. Barbara stared, mesmerized, into his gaze. Something inside her turned over as she looked down into that unusual face, compelling even in injury. "Are you an angel?" he asked softly.

20

"No, I'm your doctor," Barbara replied crisply, maintaining her professional calm although her pulse was quickened. In his dazed state Steve had been interesting and appealing. But as he began to come out of his stupor, she found him something more than that, something intriguing and potent. She pulled the thread tight and prepared to take another stitch.

Steve looked at her again. "Of course you're not an angel," he said. "Angels don't have crow's feet. Ow!" he yelped as Barbara inserted the needle into his forehead again.

"Just a minute and I'll give you another shot," Barbara volunteered as she withdrew a syringe of Novocaine from the wall cabinet and injected it into his forehead. "I'm sorry the first one wasn't strong enough." She glanced at her patient, trying to ignore the signals her body was sending her mind about him. When the drug had sufficiently numbed the wound, she resumed stitching, taking the tiniest stitches she could so that Steve's broad forehead would not be scarred in any way.

The aide left the room and Jenkens leaned forward and addressed himself to Steve. "You're one lucky bastard," he said cheerfully. "If that beam had been even one inch over, it could have crushed your skull like it did Al's leg."

Steve swore and tried to sit up, but Barbara pushed him back down firmly, allowing her hand to linger on his chest for a moment longer than was absolutely necessary. She scowled at Jenkens. "Al did not suffer a permanent injury, although I hope the company has adequate workmen's compensation. Right now, Mr. Sullivan, you are to concentrate on lying still so that I can sew you up, then I want to X-ray your head for a possible concussion. Mr. Jenkens, don't you have some phone calls to make?" Jenkens took the hint and left the room.

"You didn't have to get rid of him," Steve said. "I remember the whole thing, and I agree with him that I'm lucky. Instead of having a tart-tongued sexy doctor who just looks like an angel leaning over me, I could have the real thing!"

"Yes, I'd say you got off lightly," Barbara agreed as she

remembered the sickening angle of the lethal beam. "Did either of you see it coming?"

"No, we didn't," Steve acknowledged ruefully. "Although I heard something like wind in my ear right before everything went black." He looked at her shrewdly. "You are a sexy tart-tongued doctor, aren't you?" he asked.

"I told you that I was a doctor," Barbara replied, fighting down the annoyance she always felt when someone asked if she was really a doctor. She took another stitch, pulling together the folds of skin as accurately as she could.

"I know you're a doctor," Steve replied solemnly. "What I asked is if you were really a sexy tart-tongued doctor. There is a difference, you know." His eyes danced as he surveyed her form from the waist up as she bent over to tend to him.

"Yes, there is a difference," Barbara said out loud. And I'm not answering the other question, she added to herself as he casually inspected her breasts thrust tightly against her white blouse. Barbara felt herself grow warm at his sensual appraisal. It was a heady feeling, certainly not unpleasant. Reaching out, Steve lightly touched the soft material of the cuff where the button was missing. "Did you lose the button on the jobsite?" he asked worriedly.

"No," Barbara admitted. "I've been like this all day." She was beginning to wonder if she really needed to X-ray Steve for a possible concussion. His eyes had lost that dazed look and had taken on an almost piercing quality that intrigued her, and his conversation seemed quite lucid. I'll talk to him some more, she thought, and see if his responses make sense. Besides, she wondered, what is this man? Sensuous? Interesting? Fascinating, maybe? By talking to him, could she find out? "Jenkens said that you owned Sullivan Construction," she said out loud. "How long have you had your company?"

"I inherited a sizable legacy from my grandfather ten years ago," Steve replied as he allowed his eyes to roam at will over her oval face, making Barbara aware that he was taking in every feature. "I sank every penny into the best equipment and labor I could find, hired an architect who is practically a genius, worked every day and night—well, not every night," he amended as Barbara's expression became openly disbelieving, "for ten years, and here I am. How about you? How long have you been in practice?"

"A little over two years," Barbara said, surprised to have the tables turned on her, although she had no objection to answering the question. "I went to med school in Galveston and did my residency here in Houston."

"Is your specialty emergency medicine?" Steve inquired with genuine interest as he allowed his gaze to examine her slender waist, his hazel eyes deliberately bland.

"No, family practice," Barbara replied briskly, ignoring the quickening of her pulse in response to Steve's obvious interest in her. "I just happened to be in my office when Jenkens pounded on the door looking for help. I must admit, your man Fisk wasn't too happy about letting me go up in your elevator after you."

Steve sat upright. "You went up on that rickety thing?" he sputtered.

Barbara pushed him down firmly, again feeling the resistance of his hard wall of chest muscle. "Now, don't you go all chauvinistic on me," she warned him sternly. "Besides, if you're not careful I'll let your squeamish buddy Fisk take out these stitches." Maybe she could dispense with those X rays after all. Steve seemed lucid enough to her. And his attentions to her had certainly been subtle enough, not the ridiculous or heavy-handed passes that a man would sometimes make when he was not in full possession of his faculties. It was her own response to him that was disturbing Barbara. She had felt nothing for any of the men she had met since her divorce, and suddenly she was attracted to a man whom she did not know, a man who was not particularly handsome, and whom she was seeing in a purely professional capacity. What on earth was coming over her? She took her last stitch and cut the thread, then swabbed the wounded area with Betadine and put a light covering over it. "I want to keep you overnight for observation, since you don't live with anyone," she said.

"Now, how do you know that?" Steve inquired smoothly.

"Correction noted," Barbara replied, unreasonably disappointed. It was no business of hers if Steve did not live alone. She looked at him out of the corner of her eye. With his kind of appeal it would be strange if he did live by himself! "I assumed that you live alone, since Jenkens said that you're divorced," she added. "But since you do live with someone, you could go on home and we'll let her check you during the night."

"Camilla couldn't do that," Steve said with mock sadness.

"Camilla?" Barbara mouthed incredulously.

"She's a beagle," Steve added, laughing as Barbara scowled at him in exasperation. He had deliberately led her on, letting her think that he was with someone.

Embarrassed, she asked snidely, "Do you really have a beagle?"

"No, so I guess you get to keep me," he added innocently, aware that Barbara had understood the double meaning of his innocuous statement. He looked at her sharply as she washed her hands in the sink. "How about you? Are you married?"

Barbara whirled around in surprise. Most patients would not have asked her such a personal question. But then, most patients would have not flirted with her that way, either. She briefly debated whether or not to answer him, but decided that there was no reason not to. "I'm divorced," she said shortly. "I'll call admitting, and they'll take care of you until morning."

"Thank you, Dr.—What is your name, anyway?"

"Barbara Weimer," she replied as she walked toward the door.

"Thank you, Dr. Weimer," he said. "I'm sure we'll be seeing a lot more of each other in the future," he added as his eyes caressed her through the shirt and slacks she was wearing. "Night, Blue Eyes."

Very funny, Barbara thought as she shut the door to the cubicle. So he thinks we'll be seeing a lot more of each other! She knew, from the way he had been studying her in the cubicle, that Steve was thinking of "seeing" her, of seeing every inch of her. And damn, she wanted to "see" more of him! But it's too soon since Wayne, she protested to herself, and, besides, he's a patient. Oh, bother, why did he have to come along and shake me out of my contented routine, she groused, forgetting that just this morning she had despaired over her lack of interest in men. She wandered to the nurses' station and picked up Steve's chart. Sighing, she wrote the order for an X ray, although Steve had never really given any indication of having anything wrong. She would just feel better taking the photograph. She left the chart with the nurse on duty and walked out into the warm, muggy night. For once Barbara was not humming.

CHAPTER TWO

By the next morning Barbara's good humor was restored, and she made her hospital rounds with even more zest than usual. She saw her maternity patients first and then her medical patients, waiting until last to visit Mrs. Valdez in ICU. As she walked into Steve Sullivan's room, she noted that he had already showered and shaved, and was wearing an expensive pair of brand-new pyjamas and a matching velour robe. Even more than she had been the night before, Barbara was conscious of this man's tremendous appeal and charm, and felt herself unwillingly drawn to those qualities, although at the same time he made her feel a little uneasy. He was seated in the chair beside the bed, sipping a glass of orange juice and reading the morning paper. I wonder which of his girl friends he called to bring him all his gear, Barbara thought a trifle cynically. With his physical appeal and his money he was bound to have at least a few tucked away somewhere. He stood as Barbara entered the room, towering over her and exuding a raw animal sensuality, in spite of the bandaged forehead, that took Barbara's breath away. This was the first time since her divorce that she had found a man appealing in the least, and Barbara was astounded by her response to him.

"Ah, my beautiful Dr. Kildare." He grinned as he extended his hand.

Barbara winked and took his hand in hers, curiously enjoying the feel of his rough palm against her smooth one. "One oh-so-naive and dedicated young innocent at your service!" she teased, withdrawing her hand from his and holding it to her heart.

Steve appeared to be crestfallen. "I thought doctors knew everything about life," he said sadly.

"Don't you ever believe that!" Barbara laughed. "Seriously, Mr. Sullivan, how's the head today?"

"Please, make it Steve," he said smoothly as he perched on the edge of the bed. "It still hurts some, but not like it did last night. I must admit, I appreciated your little blue pain-killers in the wee hours of the morning."

"I'm glad they helped," Barbara said as she tilted his head this way and that, watching for signs of stiffness, then aimed a small disposable flashlight into his piercing hazel eyes, checking them for dilation. His eyes seemed to penetrate right through her, making Barbara feel that he could see into her very soul. At this close range she could see the green and brown flecks that blended to give them their particularly striking shine, and she wondered how they would look softened by passion. She was delighted to find both Steve and his beautiful eyes in such good shape. The hospital had notified her later in the evening that Steve had indeed been suffering from a slight concussion, and Barbara had ordered appropriate medication and treatment for him over the phone. She was glad that she had ordered the X-rays, after all. Pushing her hair back over her shoulder, she checked his chart and found nothing of importance written there. Sitting on the arm of the chair, she made a note on his chart and nodded her head. "I'm releasing you today to go home, but not back to work until next week." She held up her hand as he started to protest. "I know that Sullivan Construction depends on you, but you did have a slight concussion and therefore you may experience a little dizziness and disorientation for a few days. You're going to be in no shape to climb skyscrapers and even less to make critical business decisions. Do I make myself clear?"

"Very clear." Steve scowled. "And what is the company supposed to do while I recuperate? Twiddle its collective thumbs?"

Barbara met his irate scowl with one of her own. "And what does Sullivan Construction do on the occasional night you take off?" she demanded, referring to Steve's comment about not working every night.

"I leave instructions," he replied, not at all amused by her joke. Then he brightened. "That's what I'll do! My secretary can bring me my work at home! I'll send it back with her the next morning. No problem."

"That is not what I mean for you to do and you know it!" Barbara admonished him. "You need some time to recuperate." Still, she knew that nothing she could say would stop Steve from doing his work at home if he wanted to. And she could understand how he felt. Apparently, he was as dedicated to his company as she was to her practice. "Just don't get overly tired," she advised him.

Steve nodded, satisfied that Sullivan Construction would be taken care of. "And would it be all right for me to go out to dinner?" he asked innocently.

"Oh, that would be all right, as long as your date does the driving," Barbara replied.

"Super. Would you care to have dinner with me? You'll have to drive, of course."

"No," Barbara said shortly. She had half-expected this, and it was always an awkward situation. "I make it a policy never to date my patients," she added in explanation, her eyes mirroring regret. Oh, but she was tempted to abandon her policy just this once! The man was so exciting! Steve appealed to her strongly and he seemed to be equally attracted to her. So what harm could there be in a simple date? But would it stop there? Not if he found her as attractive as she found him, it wouldn't! No, she decided reluctantly, she wasn't ready for that yet.

Steve shrugged and Barbara heaved a sigh of relief tinged with more than a little disappointment. She had been afraid that Steve would push her, yet she really hated turning him down. Barbara was amazed that he had not put up more of a fight, unless he really hadn't cared that much about going, after all. "Very well," he said. "When do I come in and have these stitches out?"

"Call my receptionist for an appointment early next week." She turned to go. "And remember, you don't go back to work until I give you the go-ahead." As she left the room, she could have sworn she saw him wink his eye at her retreating form.

Mrs. Valdez was fading rapidly. Her heart monitor showed increasingly that her tired little heart was struggling to beat, but that it was just about to give up. Nevertheless, Barbara greeted her patient warmly and was rewarded with a faint smile. "My son said that my cat is doing all right, but that he misses me," the old lady said.

"I'm sure he does," Barbara said as she inquired about the old lady's level of comfort. At this point Barbara wanted to be sure that Mrs. Valdez was not suffering any pain. Although she did not believe in overmedication, she felt that the judicious use of mild medication caused no harm. On Mrs. Valdez's admission that she was uncomfortable, Barbara prescribed a mild pain-killer and reassured the little woman as best she could, without lying outright about her condition. Barbara shut the door of the room and leaned against it for a moment, saddened by the woman's rapid deterioration. She had hoped against hope that Mrs. Valdez might pull off the occasional miracle and go home one more time, but that was completely impossible now.

On the way to the office Barbara's thoughts returned to Steve Sullivan in spite of her resolve to think of other things. Her fingers had itched to tangle themselves in the sun-bleached hair that fell onto his face, and a part of her bitterly regretted having turned down his dinner invitation. Why do I find him so startlingly enticing? she wondered. He isn't as handsome as Max . . . or Wayne, she added ruefully. So what is it? Why do I respond to him the way I do? Is it sex appeal? Barbara remembered the heady feeling she had known when Steve had visually examined her so thoroughly in the emergency room, and the woman in her longed to feel that again today. Oh, wouldn't the perfume makers love to bottle and sell Essence of Sullivan! Barbara wondered about his social life with an emotion startlingly close to jealousy. Did he have a girl friend in the singular, or several in the plural? What had happened to his marriage? Did his work demand a lot out of him? Oh, Barbara, she chided herself, the next thing you're going to be picturing is what he looks like in the shower.

Without meaning to, Barbara remembered the feel of the hard muscled body under her fingers as she had run them down his body, checking him for injuries. She smiled a little and blushed furiously, even though she was alone. She could tell exactly what he looked like in the shower. She wasn't a doctor for nothing.

Barbara snipped the last suture and gently pulled the thread from the skin. "Good as new," she said brightly.

Steve sat up and slicked down the hair on the back of his head. He gently felt the injury, careful not to irritate the still-purple bruise above his eye. "I can barely feel the scar," he said thoughtfully.

"When the redness of the new tissue disappears, you probably won't be able to see it, either," Barbara reassured him . "I took the smallest stitches I could."

"For that I thank you," Steve replied solemnly. "Although I can't think why you would care what this ugly mug looks like."

"Oh, you're not ugly," Barbara replied quickly.

"Why, thank you, ma'am," Steve replied in an exaggerated drawl. Barbara ducked her head, not wanting him to see the embarrassment on her face.

"How about dinner with me tonight?" Steve asked suddenly.

"I don't date patients," she replied as she washed her hands at the sink.

"I'm not your patient anymore," Steve argued genially. "You've discharged me from your care, and the next time I get conked on the head, hopefully my regular physician will be around."

"I hope you don't get hurt again," Barbara said sincerely. "But no on the date."

30

Steve shrugged his shoulders and held out his hand. "I'm glad to have made your acquaintance," he said firmly. "Be seeing you."

Barbara stared at Steve's retreating form, desperately wishing now that she had accepted his offer. She had honestly expected him to put up more of a fight about the date. Surprised and very disappointed, she made a note on his file and handed it to Sylvia on the way to her next patient.

"Who was that fox that just walked out of here?" Sylvia drooled as she rummaged in the file cabinet for the file on Barbara's next patient.

"Steve Sullivan," Barbara replied as she tapped her fingers impatiently on the counter and pushed her hair clip roughly into her hair. Usually the office ran smoothly, but today everything had gone wrong, and this was the third time that Sylvia had been unable to find a file.

"Was he the one you treated up on the skyscraper?" Sylvia's eyes grew even larger.

"The same," Barbara replied, a little amused by Sylvia's interest and surprised to find herself on the receiving end of the questions for once. "Have you looked in the inactive file?"

"She said she was in here just a few months ago," Sylvia said as she slammed one drawer and opened another.

Barbara chewed on a fingernail and fidgeted impatiently, wanting to look for the file herself but realizing that she would have less luck than Sylvia.

"So did he ask you out? Is he married or otherwise attached?"

"Yes and no," Barbara replied absently. "Did she say what she was in here for last time?"

"Blood test," Sylvia said. "So where are you going?"

"We're not," Barbara replied dryly. "What kind of blood test?"

"She was getting married," Sylvia said. "Why aren't you going? Aren't you feeling well?"

31

"I'm feeling fine," Barbara said. "She was getting married, you said? Why don't you check under her maiden name?"

Sylvia looked dumbfounded for a moment, then searched under the girl's maiden name. Sure enough, the chart surfaced immediately. "Sorry," the girl muttered, red faced. "So why aren't you going out with him?"

"I don't date patients," Barbara said as she hurried off with the chart. Sylvia stared after her in astonishment.

Barbara saw four more patients, then sat down to an unusually long list of telephone calls. It was after six when she finally made the last call. So tired that she had to force herself up from the chair, she wondered just for a moment if medicine as a career had been a crazy choice to make. She was worn out, and her workday was far from over. Again alone in the office, she pulled her purse out of her drawer and placed her beeper inside, then slipped out of her white coat and headed out the back door. The evening reminded her of the one when Jenkens had pounded on the front door for help, but she glanced over at the skyscraper under construction and noted with disappointment that the building was silent and that there were no cars parked around it. Everyone must have gone home hours ago. She thought ruefully of the beeper she carried with her. Tonight she was taking Max's calls as well as her own, since Max was taking Marcie to a premiere movie and did not want to be interrupted. Barbara did not mind, since she owed Max a favor, but she was exhausted and did not look forward to a constantly interrupted evening.

Barbara noticed a yellow Jaguar parked in front of her Corvette, which was sitting in the deep shade of a cottonwood tree. Puzzled, since the back lot was private, she hesitated for a moment but saw no one and headed for her car with confidence. She unlocked the door and climbed in behind the wheel, then stifled a scream as Steve Sullivan reached over and took the keys from her hand.

"Damn you, you scared me to death!" she snapped when she

could get her breath back. "What are you doing sitting in my car?"

"Waiting for you," Steve said calmly. "I want you to have dinner with me."

"Why couldn't you have waited for me in the office?" Barbara said tiredly as she rubbed her hand across her forehead.

"Because in the office I would have gotten the same polite brush-off that I got this afternoon. I didn't want that. I want to take you out to dinner somewhere nice. You look like you need it."

"Thanks," Barbara replied tartly as she glanced in the mirror at her tired face and messy hair, stung by the implication and knowing he was right. "But the answer is still no."

"Well, all right," Steve said as he put her keys in his pocket and laid his head back against the headrest. "You sure keep a junky car."

"Please give me my keys," Barbara replied through clenched teeth. "I'd like to go home."

"And I'd like to take you out for a meal and get to know you better," Steve argued. "I wonder how long you are willing to sit here before you give in?"

"Until the beeper goes off for the first time," Barbara said impatiently as she smoothed her rumpled denim skirt. "Then I'll have to take my purse and go call my exchange, and hope that by the time I return you'll have come to your senses in case I have to go to the hospital in this car with those keys."

"The putting of me in my place has been duly noted," Steve said as he handed her the keys. "I didn't realize that you were still on duty, so to speak." He made no move to get out of the car. "How about this, then? There's a nice little restaurant a few blocks from here. Nothing fancy, just plain good food and the service is quick. That way, if the beeper goes off, you still get your supper, and if it doesn't, we can visit for a while."

So this is how he gets his way, Barbara thought. When a head-on collision isn't going to work, he's not above turning on the charm and cajoling his way to his goal. Barbara was irritated and at the same time amused by his tactics. But weren't you disappointed when he left this afternoon? she thought ruefully. Weren't you just crushed? You know you want to go! And she did want to go with him. She wanted to go very much, and not just because the idea of a sandwich and a round of telephone calls did not appeal. She wanted to get to know this interesting man better, to find out with her mind what her body already knew about him! She looked down at her wrinkled denim skirt and wilted yellow blouse, then over to Steve's perfectly coordinated tan knit shirt and slacks. Surely Steve did not intend to take her out dressed like this! "I'll have to go home and change," she said tiredly.

"Why?" Steve challenged. "So you're wilted. So what? You still need to eat." He grinned openly at her, but his teasing about her appearance had been gentle, not derisive as Wayne's had often been.

That gentle teasing was her undoing. "I'll go on one condition," she capitulated. "We take separate cars, and if I get a hospital call I'll go on and you can go home."

"We'll take your car," Steve compromised. "That way if you get a call, you can respond, and I'll just wait for you in the lounge. Deal?"

"Deal," Barbara replied, humming softly as she turned over the ignition.

Barbara backed her car out of the parking lot and turned to Steve. "Where do you have in mind?" she asked him brightly.

"Lucy's," he said. "Do you know the place?"

"No, but I'd love to try it," Barbara replied. "Show me the way."

Steve gave her very clear instructions, and Barbara had no trouble finding the small, cheerful restaurant. They said very little to each other on the short trip, Barbara concentrating on the fierce Houston traffic and Steve surveying the contents of her cluttered car with interest. He looked through a stack of medical

34

journals and nosed through several boxes of drug samples that the salesman always left. Carefully he removed the white coat that was slung haphazardly across the dash and laid it in the back seat. "Are you a fanatic about neat cars?" Barbara asked finally.

"How'd you ever guess?" Steve asked ruefully.

"And perfectly coordinated clothes, too," Barbara said as she eyed Steve's impeccable grooming.

"Guilty again," Steve replied blandly, eyeing Barbara's skirt and blouse with amusement.

"Well, if you intend to spend much time around me, you'll have to get used to riding around in a dump truck," Barbara said firmly, then backed away from the statement quickly, biting her lip. Whatever had possessed her to say a thing like that? How did she know whether Steve intended to spend any time at all with her after tonight?

"Since I intend to spend a lot of time with you in the future, I'll remember that," Steve said smoothly, confusing her further.

As Barbara parked her car in the small lot beside Lucy's, the familiar sharp *beep* sounded twice, then the garbled message that Barbara always had difficulty understanding was transmitted. She should have known that it would sound for her. It always did.

"What was that?" Steve asked, puzzled.

"The beeper," Barbara replied. "I'll have to find a telephone." She waited for the familiar scowl to appear on his face, as it always had on her ex-husband's. Normally she did not mind the beeper, but at this point it felt like an intrusion. She eyed Steve anxiously. Was he going to become irritated by the interruption?

"Fair enough," Steve said genially. "I'll get us a table while you make your call."

The pretty waitress showed Steve to a table while Barbara made her call from a phone booth in the lobby. A young mother was concerned because her small son had thrown up his supper. After questioning the mother carefully, Barbara decided that the

35

child had a mild case of gastroenteritis and gave the mother instructions over the telephone. She then made a second call to the pharmacy that the family used and ordered medication for the child. Barbara found her way into the dining room, glad that the problem could be dealt with over the telephone.

Steve was sipping a glass of wine and reading the menu. Barbara watched him carefully, still expecting some form of irritation to be expressed. Steve only smiled warmly and rose to seat her. "Minor problem?" he asked.

"For me, yes," Barbara replied as she looked over her menu. "A little boy with gastroenteritis."

"Sounds serious," Steve said solemnly.

"Not really," Barbara replied with a twinkle in her eye. "It just means the kid is upchucking. Another word for that is—"

"Never mind," Steve interrupted her dryly. "I know what it means."

Barbara smiled and picked up her glass of beer, sipping it delicately and licking her lips. "There's an epidemic of it going around," she said thoughtfully.

"That doesn't surprise me," Steve volunteered, brushing a strand of sun-bleached hair off his forehead. "We've had three or four workers a day out with it for the last two weeks."

"Just on the skyscraper?" Barbara asked as she reached up and adjusted her hair clip.

"Yes, just on the skyscraper," Steve replied. "Probably more on the other jobsites and in the main office."

"Just how big is your company?" Barbara asked curiously. She had thought that the skyscraper was his only job.

"I have four other buildings going up right now, although that one is the largest," Steve admitted. Barbara was impressed with the size of Steve's operation.

The waitress came to take their dinner order. Steve chose a large steak and Barbara selected an embellished hamburger with all the trimmings. Barbara took another sip of her beer and eyed

Steve thoughtfully. "Is owning your own business demanding?" she asked.

"Oh, yes," Steve replied, sipping his drink. "Some weeks I put in sixty hours or more. A lot of people depend on me for their livelihood, and others are expecting their building to be ready on time. I have some excellent employees who really help a lot, but ultimately the responsibility is mine." He shifted uncomfortably in his chair. "Sorry for the sermon," he said quickly. "Sometimes I forget myself and talk too much."

"You didn't," Barbara assured him. "Tell me," she added with her usual candor, "how do your employees like working for a workaholic?"

"I beg your pardon," Steve said firmly. "I am not a workaholic!"

"Then what would you call it?" Barbara challenged. "Sixty-hour weeks, no time for anything else . . ."

"Who said that I don't have time for anything else?" Steve laughed. "I don't always work sixty hours, and I have time for lots of other things. I work out at the gym, I hunt and fish regularly, and I read at least two mystery novels a week. I even feed pretty women dinner once in a while. I'm out tonight, aren't I?"

Barbara was amazed. "But how do you manage to do all that?"

"I make time," Steve replied. Barbara laughed out loud. "No, Barbara, I'm serious. My career is important to me, and I do a damn good job of it, but it simply does not come first in my life. I very jealously make time for other things."

"What does come first in your life?" Barbara asked. "What is that important to you?"

"I'm not sure," Steve admitted as he rattled the ice in his glass. "No one thing that I can put my finger on. I suppose that I strive to have a well-rounded life."

I have to hand it to him, Barbara thought to herself. If what Steve had said was true, and she had no reason to believe that

37

it wasn't, then he had achieved a balance in his life, a balance between the demands of his career and his other interests. "I envy you," Barbara said honestly. "I must admit that my existence is pretty single-minded sometimes."

"I don't think you can compare my situation to yours," Steve said gently. "People's lives aren't dependent on me."

True, Barbara thought. But she still thought that Steve had managed to do something quite remarkable. He had built a successful business but had not sacrificed his personal life to do it.

The waitress brought their dinner just as Barbara's beeper went off again. Shrugging her shoulders, she told Steve to go ahead and eat while she made the call. Wearily she plodded to the lobby and called her exchange. It was Netta Morris, the office hypochondriac. Usually Netta limited her indulgence to office hours, but tonight she had developed a severe headache and didn't Dr. Weimer think that it could be a sign of a brain tumor?

Biting her lip to keep from telling the woman off, Barbara assured her that a simple headache was not a sign of anything serious unless it continued. Netta had several more questions as long as she had Barbara on the line, and it was a good ten minutes before Barbara could get away. Resigned to the fact that her hamburger was probably cold, she made her way back to Steve. He was cheerfully polishing off the last of his steak, but Barbara's hamburger was nowhere to be seen.

"Where's my burger? I'm starved!" Barbara announced.

Steve signaled the waitress, who went to the kitchen and returned with Barbara's hamburger, piping hot and ready to eat.

"I was afraid it would get cold, so I had her take it back and keep it warm," Steve explained as Barbara bit in gratefully. She was simply amazed by Steve's thoughtfulness. Never once in the six years that they were married had her ex-husband Wayne tried to keep a restaurant meal fresh for her.

"Thank you," Barbara said sincerely between bites of food.

"This is delicious!" She took a forkful of delicately curled French fries.

"I've always enjoyed coming here," Steve said. "I bring my son here often. I have him every other weekend."

"You have a son?" Barbara asked in surprise. She did not associate the sexy Steve with the accoutrement of a family.

"Scooter's almost nine now," Steve said proudly. "Care to see a picture of him?" Barbara nodded, touched that Steve was obviously so fond of the child.

Barbara held the photograph that Steve got out of his wallet so that she could see it clearly. The photograph must have been a recent one, because the tall boy stood as high as Steve's chest. He had the same light-brown hair as Steve and similar facial features, but his build was considerably stockier than that of his lean father, and his eyes were a vivid blue. "What do you want to bet he's a star defensive tackle in a few years?" Barbara asked. "With a whole pep squad of girls chasing him after the game!"

"You noticed the build?" Steve asked lightly. "Yes, I'm afraid that one's going to be bigger than his old man." Steve's face sobered. "He's a good kid. In fact, he's the only thing Shelley and I ever did right."

"Shelley is your ex-wife?" Barbara asked as she returned her attention to her hamburger.

Steve nodded. "Shelley and I were married for three of the worst years you can imagine. I tried, and I think Shelley did, but we were like water and oil. We probably wouldn't have lasted for that long, but we tried to stay together for Scooter's sake. Anyway, we divorced when Scooter was two, and she's remarried to a very nice guy who I feel sorry for." Barbara laughed out loud at that, and ruefully Steve joined her. "But I have to give her credit," he added. "She's done a marvelous job of raising Scooter. She's a good mother. She was just a lousy wife."

Casually Barbara asked, "Did the long hours you have to put in bother your wife?"

Steve looked at her shrewdly for a moment, but Barbara was

busy with her hamburger and did not notice. "No, I can honestly say that they didn't," Steve said firmly. "She liked being married to an up-and-coming young businessman. The problem was strictly between us."

"And you've never wanted to marry again?" Barbara asked before she could stop herself.

"Let's just say that I have no intention of ever entering into that sort of relationship again," Steve said lightly.

Barbara heaved a sigh of relief and admitted to herself that she had been half afraid of Steve until now. She was vibrantly aware of the attraction that she felt for him, and she knew very well that he was attracted to her, too, and had been ever since she had stitched his wound in the emergency room. He had flirted with her then, and tonight she noticed the way his eyes would widen every time she walked back into the room, and the way he had subtly examined her while they talked. Oh, yes. The attraction was mutual, and if Steve felt the same way about marriage that she did, it would be all right to let their relationship develop into whatever it was going to. There would be no danger of Steve deciding that he wanted to marry her.

"How long have you been divorced?" Steve asked as Barbara devoured the last bite of her hamburger.

"It's been final for almost a year now," Barbara replied slowly, reluctant to say anything about her failed marriage or painful divorce. "I've put the mess behind me."

"What happened to your marriage?" Steve asked bluntly.

Barbara stifled her indignation quickly. Still sensitive about the reasons for her divorce, she reminded herself that Steve, and others like him who had been divorced for a long time, probably thought nothing of discussing their divorces with their friends. Yet she was reluctant to tell Steve the whole messy story. Hedging, she said quietly, "Let's just say that the marriage should have never been. Wayne and I had some pretty important circumstances against us, and neither of us had the wisdom to deal

40

with those circumstances. Wayne has made a happy second marriage, and I wish him well."

"It still hurts you like hell, doesn't it?" Steve asked astutely.

"Yes," Barbara said frankly. "But I'm getting over it."

"Good!" Steve said enthusiastically. "I'll admit," he went on slowly, "it took me a while to get over mine." Much to Barbara's relief he asked her no more about her breakup, realizing that the topic was one that she did not care to talk about.

Steve and Barbara chatted cheerfully as Barbara finished her hamburger and the waitress cleared their plates. They discovered a mutual interest in tennis, Steve playing regularly at the country club and Barbara playing against other doctors whenever she could. They agreed to a match sometime in the future, and she wondered if they had any other interests in common. She certainly hoped so! Steve mentioned again his love of books and said that he haunted secondhand bookstores in order to feed his habit. Barbara admired Steve's passion for reading and admitted to herself that she missed the light reading she had done before she became a doctor. Now it seemed that all she ever had time for was medical journals, and she promised herself to read at least a part condensation of one of the latest mystery thrillers so she could discuss it intelligently with him.

The waitress appeared with coffee and apple pie about the time Barbara's beeper went off again. She eyed Steve enviously as he dug into his pie, and trudged into the lobby to place her call. This one came from Memorial, and with a sinking feeling Barbara heard from the ICU nurse that Mrs. Valdez was failing rapidly and could Dr. Weimer come on down?

So much for the apple pie, Barbara thought as she rushed back into the dining room. "That was from the hospital," she said as Steve swallowed the last of his pie. "I have to go down there. Damn!" she added suddenly. "You don't have a car here."

"And you don't have time to take me back to the office," Steve added. "No problem. You can drop me off after you deal with your patient."

41

"This is going to take a while, Steve," Barbara said quietly. "I have a patient in ICU who probably won't last the night. I may be very late. You better take a cab." She raked her fingers through her hair impatiently as Steve signaled for the bill. The waitress handed him the check and a paper sack. Steve took Barbara's hand firmly in his and led her to the cashier, where he rushed through payment, and followed her to the car. Barbara followed him, wondering what was in the sack that the waitress had handed him.

When they reached the car, Steve held out his hand. "I'll drive," he said firmly.

"What?" Barbara asked peevishly. "I prefer to do my own driving, thank you."

"I said I'll drive," he said as he took the keys from her hand, unlocked the passenger door, and pushed her inside. He handed her the sack and slammed the door shut.

A little put out, Barbara peeked into the sack and was astonished to find a piece of cellophane-wrapped apple pie and a plastic fork. Gingerly she removed the cellophane and then quickly she took a bite of the delicious pie. She was downing her second mouthful when Steve slid in behind the wheel and started the engine.

"Thanks for the pie," she said brightly, her earlier anger at his arrogance forgotten. "It was extremely thoughtful of you."

Steve looked at her and smiled faintly. "You have a long evening ahead," he said solemnly. "I wanted to be sure that you had enough food in you to carry you through it."

Thoroughly amazed that Steve would even think of such a caring thing, Barbara could only nod as she stared into the traffic and ate her dessert.

CHAPTER THREE

As she strode into ICU, Barbara knew that Mrs. Valdez would never make it through the night. The frail little woman had become even thinner during her week in the hospital, and now was barely a ripple under the sheet. The sharp little tongue had said nothing that made sense all day, and the electrocardiograms showed a heart that by all normal standards should already have stopped beating. Her son, a solid, middle-aged man, was holding one of her hands and her daughter-in-law was holding the other. Both were crying silently. Barbara read the chart and examined the electrocardiograms and shook her head. There was nothing more that she could do. Mrs. Valdez was at the point where any further medical intervention would only prolong and agonize her death.

Barbara sighed and perched on a stool. Now it was a matter of time. Mrs. Valdez shifted and the electrocardiogram bounced for a moment, then returned to its weak pattern. "Does that mean anything, Dr. Weimer?" Mr. Valdez asked anxiously.

"No," Barbara said softly, and motioned for Mr. Valdez to join her out in the hall. "I want to be honest with you," Barbara said compassionately. "I seriously doubt that your mother will make it until morning."

Mr. Valdez nodded his head. "Sí, I know that. But it is better that she go peacefully."

Barbara nodded. "I'm glad you feel that way. A lot of families want me to keep their loved one alive at any price, when it is better to let him or her go with dignity." She and Mr. Valdez returned to his mother, and Barbara interceded with the dutiful ICU nurse who insisted that the Valdezes' time was up. "Let them stay," Barbara said sharply. "It will be their last chance to be with her."

Mercifully, Mrs. Valdez died in her sleep about eleven. Barbara checked her one last time and spoke with her son again, who thanked Barbara for the care his mother had received. He confided that the old lady had not been happy about seeing a lady doctor for the first time, but that later she had become convinced that Barbara was the best little doctor in Houston. Smiling faintly through her tears, Barbara left the family. She would miss the old lady's periodic office visits and tart opinions. Although Barbara had grown accustomed to losing patients, it still hurt, especially when those patients were also her friends.

Wiping her eyes, she found Steve where she had left him, in one of the comfortable lounges. He had obviously visited the gift shop in the lobby, since he was immersed in the latest best-selling thriller. She cleared her throat and he jumped up and closed the book, carefully dog-earing his page. When he saw the tears on her face, he immediately withdrew a handkerchief from his pocket and wiped her brimming blue eyes. "I gather you lost your patient?" he said quietly.

Barbara nodded and sniffed. "But I knew that going in there."

"That doesn't make it hurt any less," Steve replied gently. "Are you ready to go?"

Barbara nodded and led the way to her car. Steve handed her the keys, but before she could start the engine he laid his hand on her arm and turned her to face him. The touch of his hand on hers was curiously exciting and soothing. "Forgive me if I'm being presumptuous," he said, "but I get the feeling that you might need to talk about what happened in there tonight. There's a nice little bar a few blocks from here if you'd care to go there."

"It's late," Barbara protested automatically. She bit her lip. One part of her would dearly love to talk to Steve about losing Mrs. Valdez, about losing any patient. But she had never had anyone to talk to about such things before, and she was not sure she wanted to start now. Wayne had never listened to her, and this man's offer to talk about it caught her off guard. Yet she was sorely tempted. It might do her good to get some of it off her chest.

As though sensing her indecision, Steve encouraged her gently. "I'm not sleepy, if that's what's stopping you. How about you?"

"No, I'm not sleepy. All right," Barbara said as she shook her hair free from the loose ponytail that she had automatically tied in ICU. "Point the way."

"I'm glad you wear your hair free," Steve volunteered. "Too many women with beautiful hair feel obligated to cut it or pin it up. A man could get lost in that hair of yours."

Barbara started to say something, but thought better of it. What could she say to a statement like that? Warmed by his praise, she turned on the ignition and turned to Steve. "Point the way," she repeated.

The bar that Steve selected was smoky but quiet. A few people were sitting on barstools listening to the piano player, but most of the tables were empty and Steve and Barbara sat in a booth away from the main room. A barmaid took their order and Steve turned to Barbara, clasping her hand in his. The touch of his rough-palmed hand across the table sent tingles up Barbara's arm and warmed her. She was physically attracted to him and glad of it, glad that Wayne had not deprived her of the ability to feel! Shaken, Barbara forced her thoughts back to why Steve had brought her here, and her expressive face mirrored her conflicting feelings about facing death each day.

"Tonight wasn't all that bad," Barbara began slowly as she rubbed her forehead thoughtfully. Steve nodded with interest, his rugged face thoughtful. "Mrs. Valdez was old and it was time for her to go. And her family was ready to let her go. It's much worse if the family wants me to take heroic measures when none are called for."

45

"Then, why the tears?" Steve asked gently. "If it was no worse than you say."

"Because I lost a friend tonight as well as a patient," Barbara explained. "Mrs. Valdez has been coming to me ever since I opened my practice. I actually looked forward to her appointments because I really liked her. And I found out tonight from her son that she felt the same way about me. That meant a lot."

"And so you cried," Steve added. "Tell me, if I had been dead up on that skyscraper, would you have been upset?"

"No, not like with Mrs. Valdez," Barbara said honestly. "I didn't know you then. But I might have thought it was a waste."

"A waste?" Steve asked.

"Sure. You were obviously young and healthy, and presumably living life to the fullest, and if you had lost all that . . ." Barbara trailed off uncertainly, shuddering visibly. It had come so close to happening to him!

Steve stared at her strangely as he interpreted her shudder. "I just almost bought it up there," he said slowly. "I honestly hadn't thought about it before now, but I could have died."

"Well, don't," Barbara returned crisply. "I see a lot more near misses than I do hits!"

"But it does bother you when you lose a patient that you have treated and that you are fond of," Steve probed. The waitress brought Steve's bourbon and Barbara's wine.

Barbara took a sip of her wine before answering. "Sure it does," she admitted. "That person is your friend. And it hurts even worse when it's someone who could have lived for a lot longer. Just last month I lost a ten-year-old in a damned car accident. I fought for three days to save him and I couldn't. That hurt."

"Did it hurt because of the boy, or because you felt that you failed?"

Barbara shook her head admiringly at Steve's perception. "Now, how did you guess?" she asked softly as she sipped her wine. "Most of it is honest grief for the patient, but yes, there

46

is a definite sense of failure when I can't save one, especially if the treatment involved a lot of critical decisions on my part. Sometimes I go over it in my mind for days, wondering, if I had done this or that differently, if it would have made a difference. Most of the time the outcome would probably have been the same, but how do I know that? And then sometimes the family blames you, even if just subconsciously."

"Are other doctors as sensitive as you are?" Steve asked.

"It depends on the doctor," Barbara admitted. "Some, cancer specialists, for example, know they are going to lose many of them, so they get a little hardened to it. Others who don't see it very often in their field will go into a depression for days when it happens to them. I guess for a family-practice physician, I'm more sensitive than most."

"Then, why on earth did you go into that field of medicine?" Steve asked in bafflement. "Why not an impersonal specialty?"

"Because I wanted the involvement," Barbara explained, a soft smile on her tired face. "You see, the happy outweighs the sad any day. For every patient I lose, I send home dozens more who are healthier and happier than they were when they came. And then I have the joy of bringing them into the world, also." She took another sip of wine and brushed a strand of hair off her face. "Steve, I chose family practice on purpose, so I could become involved. I didn't want to be like the specialists who refer to their patients as 'the gallbladder in 109' or 'the triple bypass I did yesterday.'"

"And so you have to take the sad with the happy," Steve said thoughtfully as he rubbed his chin. "Tell me, who do you normally talk to about your feelings?"

"No one," Barbara replied honestly.

"You don't ever talk to anyone about this?" Steve asked disapprovingly.

Barbara shook her head. "No, never," she admitted frankly.

Steve frowned at her. "Tell me, then, how do you usually cope with these feelings?"

47

Barbara shrugged. "I usually don't, I guess," she admitted. "Or if it's really bad, I might have a good cry on the way home."

"Why haven't you talked to anyone before now?" Steve demanded, his hazel eyes almost accusing.

Irritation briefly passed across Barbara's features, to be replaced by a look that was decidedly wistful. "Because there's never been anybody to talk to before," she said simply.

"All right, Dr. Weimer, hear this. From now on, anytime you need someone to talk to about something like this, you are to call me any hour of the day or night. I might not know much about medicine, but I do know about people. Believe it or not, you learn a lot about people in construction work," he added. "So you come to me. All right?"

"I can't impose on you like that!" Barbara protested. "What if the next time it's at three in the morning?"

"That's all right," Steve insisted. "Now, I want your promise."

"All right," Barbara capitulated. "I promise." She looked across the table at Steve with a sense of wonder. How could a man that she barely knew make such a generous offer? Was it just a come-on? Heaven only knew, sometimes she did desperately need someone to talk to. Wayne had never shown the least interest in her work or the joys and sorrows that went with it, and her family and friends led their own lives and really wouldn't have understood. Yet Steve seemed to know instinctively that sometimes she just needed to talk about something that had happened in her work. And he had offered to be that someone. She looked him in the eye and saw the sincerity there and felt a tremendous sense of relief. It hadn't been a come-on, an easy way for him to gain her trust. He really meant it. Grateful, Barbara finished her wine and smiled across the table at Steve. "It's late," she said finally. "We'd better go."

A slight breeze ruffled their hair on the way to the car. They walked slowly, hand in hand, each loath to end the strange evening that they had spent together. Barbara unlocked the car and slid inside, then leaned over and unlocked the passenger door so that Steve could get in. She looked at him expectantly, wondering if he was going to kiss her. She wanted him to. He was the first man since Wayne whom she had felt anything for, and she longed for the feel of his mouth on hers. Steve looked into her eyes for a moment, then turned away and began fumbling with his seat belt. Confused and rejected, Barbara started the engine and drove back to her office in the late-night traffic. What did she expect, for heaven's sake? It was just a casual date. She had obviously misread the signs of his interest in the restaurant. Maybe she did not really attract him in that way.

She parked the car out of habit in the space allotted to her, and unbuckled her seat belt and extended her hand. "Thank you for the evening," she said haltingly. "I'm sorry it couldn't have been better for you."

"You silly woman," Steve rumbled, "it couldn't have been any better for me!" His arm snaked out and wrapped itself around her waist, pulling her across the seat slowly until her lips were just a few inches from his own. "I told myself I wasn't going to do this, that you were upset, but I can't stop myself!" Without giving Barbara a chance to protest, he bent his lips forward and claimed hers.

The kiss was hard and passionate, startling them both with its searing intensity. Steve thrust his tongue into Barbara's receptive mouth and tangled it into hers, causing a low moan of pleasure to rise from her throat. She slid her hands around Steve's neck and clenched a fistful of his hair in her hand, curling and uncurling her fingers in the thick brown mane, feeling the hair bounce back in her hand. His hands came up and tangled in the long platinum tresses, caressing Barbara's head and throat with a gentle pressure and sending waves of pleasure down her back. "I've wanted to do that since the first time I saw you," Steve admitted as he pulled away from her mouth momentarily. "I saw you from the skyscraper. You were going up the steps into the

49

back door and that hair was blowing in the wind. Don't ever cut it, Barbara."

Barbara nodded her head and impelled his mouth back to her own, eager to continue her exploration of this sensual man who had singled her out tonight and cajoled her into accepting his company. Steve was bringing her alive again after a long dormancy, and she thrilled to his sensitive touch. She moved even closer to him, longing for a more intimate union, sliding her arms around his waist and with eager fingers kneading the tough muscles that she had once before felt so impersonally. But never again would she be able to touch this man without emotion. He was setting her aflame and she was loving every minute of it. Delicately, tenderly, Steve ran his hands down her face and throat and over her breasts, feeling the nipples swell and harden from his touch. Slowly, tantalizingly, he undid the top buttons of her blouse and slipped his hand inside, finding her generous breast and enclosing it in his fingers. Stunned by the pleasure coursing through her body, Barbara instinctively thrust herself closer to him, gasping when he circled her nipple through the sheer lace bra that she wore. She lifted the hem of his knit shirt and ran her hands through the thick hair on his stomach, delighting in the feel of his quivering muscles.

After what seemed like a moment but surely had been longer, Steve pulled away and buttoned her shirt. "Nothing would please me more than to kiss you and hold you all night," he murmured, "but it is late and we have to work tomorrow."

Barbara reluctantly pulled down his shirt. "You're right," she said slowly, fighting to regain her composure.

Steve took her chin in his hand. "I want to see you this weekend," he said insistently.

"I'd love to, but I have the beeper," she said apologetically. "It would be just like tonight."

"I didn't think tonight was too bad," Steve said with a raised eyebrow. Barbara blushed with pleasure and embarrassment at his statement. "The beeper won't bother me. I just want to see you."

"We'll see," Barbara hedged, not because she did not want to see him again, but because she would be saddled with the beeper and the constant interruptions that it represented. She did not want her time with Steve to be at the mercy of her practice. She wanted to be with Steve alone. She watched Steve as he got out of her car and into his, then as he revved his motor and drove away into the night. Oh, yes, she wanted to see him again, of that she was very sure. So maybe this would be her serious romantic involvement, she thought. Barbara covered her throbbing lips with her hand and smiled, feeling her lips curl into her palm. Yes, she could still feel for a man. She certainly felt a lot for Steve Sullivan!

Barbara swirled the amber wine around in the long-stemmed wineglass and stared at her half-eaten supper. Although she had skipped lunch, she was not particularly hungry and her small steak sat congealing in its own juice. She glanced around the living room. The professionally decorated room was messy as usual, and she supposed that she ought to pick up a little before the maid arrived in the morning to do the heavier cleaning, but she was tired and frankly the clutter did not bother her that much. Instead, Barbara pulled her old cotton robe over her knees and stared out the window at the bright Houston skyline, framed by the window of her new condominium. It had been three days since Steve had taken her out, and when he had called her the next day, she had agreed to another date with him on the following Friday. At the time it had seemed like a good idea, but now Barbara was not so sure. She had sworn that she would give herself plenty of time to recover from the painful and bitter divorce, and it had been less than a year since the breakup. She knew that a relationship with Steve Sullivan would not remain superficial for long, and Barbara was not sure that she was ready to risk the vulnerability that came with intimacy. She had loved and trusted a man once, and had been hurt very badly by the deterioration of that partnership. Was she ready for another relationship? Another marriage? Barbara knit her fingers together in agitation. No, she thought. Definitely not another marriage!

The last of the light in the western sky faded, leaving only the artificial light of streetlamps and shopwindows and traffic to illuminate the night sky. Barbara ran her fingers through her long hair and permitted herself to think of the man whom she was trying to forget, and in fact was forgetting, but who had left his scars on her spirit. Somewhere out there Wayne Jameson, Barbara's ex-husband, and his new wife were probably rushing to a political meeting or entertaining one of Wayne's wealthy clients in their perfectly groomed suburban home or attending a lavish party with all of Houston's other up-and-coming young attorneys. And Marsha would be fresh and beautifully dressed and have not a hair out of place, the perfect accessory for a man in Wayne's position. Barbara sighed and tugged on her hair gently. She wondered if Marsha had been eager to take her place as Mrs. Wayne Jameson, or if Wayne had courted Marsha and worn down her resistance in the same way he had worn down Barbara's so long ago. Barbara had decided early on in her schooling that she would be much wiser to wait until she had finished her training before embarking on marriage, and then Wayne had come along and persuaded her to change her mind.

"I want to marry you now, Barbara," he had insisted firmly at the end of her third year of medical school. "Not in five or ten years when you think you have time for me."

"But, Wayne," she had protested, "I have one more year of medical school, internship, and three years of residency facing me. It will be five or ten years, if ever, before I can be the kind of wife you need."

"That's ridiculous," Wayne had said firmly. "I want you, and I want to marry you now, not in a half-dozen years when you might decide that you're ready."

"But what about your job? My school?"

"Don't think, Barbara, just do it." And she had. She had married at the end of her junior year in medical school, and before too long it became clear that both of them should have thought harder about their union.

Problems surfaced almost immediately. Barbara began her senior year of medical school in Galveston and Wayne began his law practice in Houston, making the hour-long drive to and from Houston five, sometimes six days a week to the firm that had hired him. Barbara attended classes the better part of the day and studied late into the night, leaving very little time to spend with Wayne. The apartment was usually messy, much to Wayne's disgust, and neither one of them had time to do more than make sandwiches when they finally did get home. What little social life they shared the first year evolved around the tightly knit medical-school circle, where Wayne rightly felt that he was distinctly left out. Barbara lived for the day that she finally passed her last comprehensive exam and could move with Wayne to Houston, where he would be closer to his job, and she would start her internship at the prestigious Memorial Hospital. She had fervently hoped that the quarreling and the feelings of distance between them would go away.

If anything, the move to Houston only aggravated the problems in the marriage. Barbara immediately was plunged into her internship. She no longer had to study late into the night, but she was at the hospital over one hundred hours a week and spent one night out of three in the interns' quarters. Wayne in the meantime was making extraordinary progress in his firm, handling more and more important cases and finding it necessary to entertain often and attend important business and social functions on an increasingly frequent basis. On most of these occasions Wayne was expected to include his wife.

Barbara shifted her legs and fought the feeling of failure that threatened to swamp her whenever she remembered this portion of her life. She had tried hard. She would get home from the hospital and leave in less than an hour for a party, or dinner out with a client, or she would try to have someone over for dinner on one of her few days off. But, much to Wayne's chagrin, she did not have time to shop for a perfect wardrobe and was seldom dressed as flawlessly as the other wives were, and she found their inane chatter difficult, so she usually wound up in the corner nursing a drink. And her lack of entertaining skill and culinary talent made the few dinner parties that she tried to give a total disaster. And as the year went by more and more of the engagements were falling on evenings when she was on duty, or she had just come off a thirty-six-hour stretch at the hospital, and she simply could not get to those at all. Wayne complained bitterly about her failings and she argued with him more and went out less. The situation continued into her residency, compounded even further by the introduction of the beeper, the bane of the doctor's night out, into her life. Now she could be called out from a social occasion at a moment's notice, often leaving a furious Wayne cooling his heels in the waiting room while she tended a patient.

Barbara sighed as she picked up her plate and headed for the kitchen, putting her dishes into the already full sink and feeding her steak to Bluebonnet, her Lhasa Apso. Bluebonnet greedily gobbled the steak and scratched on the back door. The little dog had been a parting gift from Wayne, and Barbara had found her a solace in the lonely year since the divorce.

We shouldn't have let it go on so long, Barbara said to herself as she sat back down on the sofa. We should have let the relationship go before so much bitterness built up. The situation worsened as Barbara continued with her residency and Wayne's law practice grew. He began putting pressure on her to start a family, not understanding that she did not even have time most days to load the dishwasher and run a load of clothes. Wayne frequently attended his various social functions without her, or he took along his pretty secretary Marsha as his partner. Barbara was so caught up in her new practice that she did not realize that Marsha was becoming much more than Wayne's secretary and social hostess until the afternoon that she had gone by Wayne's office and surprised Wayne and Marsha in a torrid embrace. In the heated battles that followed, Wayne accused Barbara of abdicating her position as his wife in favor of her career, and said that Barbara should never have married, since she already had a husband—the M.D. behind her name.

Although Barbara had certainly catalogued Wayne's faults for him in detail, she was afraid that his words about her conduct as a wife did have some validity. She realized that Marsha had not been the problem with her marriage. Wayne's involvement with his pretty secretary had only been a symptom of a much deeper problem between the two of them, and it was not the affair that had put an end to their union. Barbara could even have forgiven the affair if their marriage had been worth saving, but sadly the relationship between her and Wayne was just too far gone to salvage.

In the long months since the divorce Barbara had agonizingly examined her part in the disaster that had been her marriage and had come to the conclusion that in fact she had put her career before her marriage and her commitment to Wayne. It was not because she had not loved Wayne. She had loved him dearly in the beginning. She had put him second not out of a lack of caring, but because her chosen profession was so demanding. But I have to put medicine first, she reminded herself over and over. People's lives depend on me, and if I'm less than one hundred percent, I could endanger a patient or even kill him outright.

Realizing the extent to which she had to be devoted to her career and still hurting from the broken relationship, Barbara had vowed that she would give herself time to recover from the trauma before she allowed herself to become emotionally involved with someone else. Until Steve Sullivan had barged into her life, she had found the waiting easy. But now she felt the void sharply. A career, no matter how fulfilling, simply could not take the place of warmth and caring in Barbara's life.

Barbara stood up and pressed her hot forehead against the

55

cool windowpane and stared out into the night. She missed having a relationship. Not just the physical intimacy, but the closeness of mind and spirit that she and Wayne had shared at one time, although that closeness had ended long before they broke up. Was it the marriage that had ruined the relationship? Barbara asked herself. She and Wayne had been so close before they had married. Was it the obligations that had come with being husband and wife that had driven them apart? Barbara had tortured herself with that question many times before without coming to a conclusion, and tonight was no different. She simply did not know. Perhaps she could not do justice to a husband and her career at the same time. And there was no way that she was going to risk another failure to find out! She did not think her spirit could stand another such blow. No, marriage was definitely out as far as Barbara was concerned.

So where does that leave me? Barbara wondered as she picked up a medical journal and flipped through it. None of the articles particularly interested her, and before too long she was staring into space again, thinking about Steve Sullivan and wondering where and how he would fit into the scheme of her life. Barbara was honest enough to admit to herself that she did not want to swear off men for good. Her physical response to Steve was proof enough of that! Yet marriage was out, and Barbara was simply too reserved and fastidious to indulge in casual sex or meaningless affairs. She wanted to have a steady, meaningful relationship, loving but without the obligations and expectations that came with a formal union. An affair, as her mother would put it. Barbara scratched a mosquito bite on her leg as a vision of Steve's face drifted across her mind. Was it too soon to let herself care again? And did she want to care about Steve?

A slight smile passed across Barbara's lips as she thought about their date, and she marveled again at both Steve's patience with the interruptions and his thoughtfulness after her patient had died. She admitted to herself that a lot of the attraction between them was physical, but realized with gratitude that she also liked and respected Steve as a person. He was patient and thoughtful about the demands of her career, and did not feel threatened by her commitment to her profession. Barbara yawned and stretched her arms above her head. Apparently, he was not any fonder of the institution of marriage than she was, yet she knew instinctively that he avoided a promiscuous lifestyle the same as she did. Yes, by God, this is the one, Barbara thought suddenly as she plopped her feet firmly on the floor and stood up. This was the right man, and they could have an affair. And Steve Sullivan would be the perfect man to have a love affair with! She would share with him the caring and the intimacy that she craved, yet she would not be bound by the obligations that came with being married to him, nor would he have to risk the same failure that he had known in the past. Steve Sullivan was the perfect candidate. She could not have done any better if she had asked Santa Claus to bring him to her! Suddenly hungry, she marched over to the refrigerator and helped herself to a big bowl of vanilla ice cream.

CHAPTER FOUR

Barbara looked at the plump young woman and fought to control her irritation. "Miss Langly, I never prescribe diet pills. I'm sorry if you think that makes me unaccommodating, but I feel that they aren't safe."

Margo Langly tossed her brunette tresses and scowled. Barbara eyed her thoughtfully. The woman was not obese by a long way, but she was carrying about twenty extra pounds that blurred the lines of what would have been a spectacular figure. Obviously a successful career woman, she seemed used to getting her own way and was appalled by Barbara's refusal to prescribe diet pills to her. "Well, if you won't prescribe them to me, then I'll find a doctor who will!"

"Be my guest," Barbara said blandly, giving in and rubbing her aching head. It was Friday, and in just a little while she would finish with her patients and her telephoning. This was her weekend with the beeper, so she could not look forward to a particularly peaceful two days, a fact that she was sure was contributing to the headache. Continuing with Margo Langly, she reached into the drawer and pulled out several leaflets about weight loss and dieting. "Miss Langly, I think it would be just wonderful if you did lose some weight. You would look better, and you would feel better about yourself. But diet pills are not the way to do it. They stimulate the central nervous system and suppress the appetite by making you high all the time. They teach you nothing about proper diet or maintaining your weight after the loss. In my experience most people who use diet pills gain their excess pounds back as soon as they go off the pills and sometimes more. I would rather have my patients go on a reasonable diet that will help them maintain the loss later."

Margo's lips set in a petulant line. "But I want the pills," she said firmly.

"Well, if your mind is made up, I suggest that you make an appointment with my partner," Barbara said resignedly. "Dr. Vaughan does prescribe them, and he will supervise you carefully."

"Very well, I'll do that," the exasperated woman said shortly. Clutching her expensive bag in her carefully manicured hands, she exited the office regally and stopped by the desk to make an appointment with Max. Barbara sighed as she made her way to her last patient. Was she too rigid in her attitude about diet pills and other crutches that some of her patients wanted? She refused to prescribe tranquilizers on a regular basis also, encouraging her patients to find nonchemical ways to deal with their problems, and this refusal often cost her a patient. No, she said to herself. Margo Langly, and all the others like her, would do better to face their problems, and then either solve them or learn to live with them.

Barbara saw her last patient and then made her telephone calls. She picked up the beeper and thrust it into her purse. How long before it goes off? she asked herself wearily. Dragging her feet, she left the office and locked the door behind her, immediately spotting the Jaguar parked beside her Corvette, Steve perched on the hood. Oh, no, she thought, he expects me to go out with him tonight! She had not completely forgotten about their tentative arrangements to see each other this weekend, but her hectic week and today's blinding headache had pushed the thought from her mind. How would he react if she begged off? Would he pout, or get angry? As she wearily approached her car, Steve's bright smile faded to a look of compassion. "You look like you got run over by one of my trucks," he said gently.

"I feel like it, too," Barbara admitted as she rubbed her sore neck. "Today was one of those," she said ruefully.

They stood silent for a moment, each sizing the other up. Whereas Barbara was definitely tired and grubby from her day at the office, Steve was freshly showered and shaved and had on crisp denims and a checkered shirt. She was delighted to note that the bruising above his eye had almost gone. Steve in turn noted the exhausted look on Barbara's face and the pain furrows around her eyes. He reached out to her face just as she reached out to touch his scar, and they caressed one another gently with sensitive fingers. His cut had healed nicely and his skin was smooth and firm and warm to the touch, and Barbara wished she had the freedom to extend her hand upward and smooth the sun-bleached brown hair. Steve did run his fingers through her hair, fresh and bouncy in contrast with the rest of her appearance. He ran his finger under her eye and traced the circle there, deeper than usual tonight.

"I was going to take you out again," Steve said slowly, "but something tells me that's the last thing you want or need to do tonight."

"I'm sorry, Steve," she said regretfully, quite disappointed. And she had so looked forward to seeing him again! But she would be the worst possible companion tonight, tired and frustrated and not looking forward to having the beeper all weekend. It just wasn't fair to inflict that on Steve. Some of her disappointment must have shown in her face, because Steve smiled enigmatically. "I won't have the beeper next weekend. Can we do something then?" she asked hopefully.

Steve nodded. "What will you do tonight?" he asked.

"Eat a sandwich and answer the telephone," Barbara said frankly.

Steve started to say something but thought better of it. With a cheerful "See you around," he hopped into the Jaguar and drove off. Barbara stared after him wistfully. If only she had not been so horribly tired! It just didn't seem fair! Shrugging her shoulders, she climbed into her car and drove to her condominium. She checked the mail and let Bluebonnet out, then walked wearily into her plushly decorated bedroom and kicked off her shoes, where they landed next to two other pairs in the middle of the floor. She pushed an unfolded load of clothes from the bed into the white velvet chair and sat down on the bed. Tiredly she stared around at the messy but opulent room, decorated in rich shades of aqua and white, and dominated by a huge brass bed. It had been her gift to herself after the divorce, in part reflecting her deeply feminine nature, and in part a small rebellion against the years of scrimping she had endured with Wayne. She unbuttoned her blouse and stripped it from her body, and the rest of her clothes quickly followed suit. Then she drew a hot bath and filled it with fragrant oil, indulging in the soothing warmth. At last she turned on the shower and washed her hair, although it was already clean. Then, thoroughly refreshed, she climbed from the tub and slowly toweled her body dry as she examined her form in the mirror, smiling at it approvingly.

Barbara was one of the few people who was completely comfortable with her body. Perhaps her years of medical training had something to do with it. She had seen hundreds of people in the unclothed state, and without vanity knew that her body was, although not perfect, certainly more attractive in the nude than most. Her limbs were long and graceful, her stomach flat, her breasts high and full. She ran her hand down the flat of her stomach as she thought of how Steve's body felt under her fingers, how he would look naked. Damn! Why had she been so tired tonight? He had wanted to pursue their courtship, and she had been too tired even to go out on a simple date. What a stupid waste! Another spasm of pain closed around her head, and listlessly she plodded to the bedroom and pulled on her old cotton robe. She was wrapping a towel around her wet hair when the doorbell pealed. "Now, who can that be?" she muttered in irritation as she answered the ringing summons.

"I decided that you needed better than a sandwich," Steve said as Barbara stared at him in astonishment. He was holding a paper bag from a local grocery, out of which peeked a head of lettuce and the top of a sack of dinner rolls. "Are you going to let me in, or stand there with your mouth open all night?"

Wordlessly Barbara stood aside and let Steve enter. Without asking the way, he strode confidently into her kitchen and dropped the sack unceremoniously on the counter. He poked around until he found her broiling pan and reached into the sack and retrieved two thick steaks. He seasoned them and placed them under the broiler, then turned back to Barbara, who was still standing stunned in the door of the kitchen. "What made you change your mind?" she asked finally.

"Just what I said," Steve replied patiently. "You needed better than a sandwich. Have you taken anything for that headache yet?"

"How did you know I have a headache?" Barbara asked suspiciously.

"I don't have to be a doctor to see the pain around your eyes. Now, go take something for the head and lie down on the couch. I'll have your supper in a few minutes."

"But . . . but you can't just walk in and take over!" Barbara sputtered indignantly. "This is my house! I'm the hostess, I'm supposed to entertain you! Besides, how did you know where the kitchen is?"

"I already have taken over," Steve replied calmly. "And I knew my way to the kitchen because I built the condos. Now, behave yourself and go do as I told you."

What an arrogant man! Barbara thought crossly. She stomped to the bathroom and found the bottle of mild pain medication she used for her occasional headaches. She swallowed two, then looked in the mirror and realized that she had greeted Steve in a rather revealing robe, no makeup, and her wet hair wrapped up in a towel. Momentarily Barbara felt embarrassed, then she shrugged her shoulders. Steve had probably seen many women in deshabille. Still, she pulled on an old pair of jeans and a stretch top, and unwound her hair from the towel. Grabbing her brush, she returned to the living room and sat on her couch, intending to brush out the snarls, but she laid her head back against the cushion and, without realizing it, shut her eyes.

Barbara sat up automatically to the sound of the ringing telephone. "Dr. Weimer here," she said crisply.

It was her exchange. Realizing that she would probably be home, the operator had dialed her number before resorting to the beeper and now gave her the number of Janet Barclay, a young mother-to-be who was due any day. Oh, please God, she thought, not tonight.

Dave Barclay sounded cheerful on the telephone. "Janet is having a few contractions," he said with anticipation. "Should we go on down?"

"Oh, no, not yet." Barbara laughed. "She may not go into labor for two or three days."

"Oh," Dave replied, disappointed.

"But I want you to know that it really is any minute now," Barbara continued seriously, the visual gap of the telephone disguising her amused smile from Dave. "No out-of-town trips for her, and don't get too far away from a telephone. Now, call me when the pains are well established and strong, as we discussed before. All right?"

"Yes, ma'am," the father-to-be replied. "Thanks, Dr. Weimer."

"I've never seen anyone come out of a sound sleep so quickly at the ringing of a phone," a voice said behind her.

Barbara whirled around, momentarily terrified. "Who? What? Oh, Steve, I forgot that you were here!" she exclaimed. "Have I been asleep long? Is your supper ruined?" She was mortified. How could she have gone to sleep that way?

"You've been asleep about forty-five minutes, and no, dinner is not ruined. When I realized that you had gone to sleep, I took the steaks off the grill and put the salad in the refrigerator. I'll put everything back on now."

"Oh, Steve, I'm sorry!" Barbara said ruefully. She scrambled off the couch and followed him into the kitchen, where Steve was putting supper back into motion.

"You don't have to apologize," Steve said as he tore up the leafy lettuce. "You were exhausted. And, anyway, now I know that you sleep with your mouth shut and that you don't snore."

"That's always nice to know," Barbara said quickly to hide her embarrassment. Seeing her asleep, Steve had seen her at her most vulnerable. At her look of chagrin he unsuccessfully fought a smile. He knows I'm embarrassed, darn him, Barbara thought, and then she gave in to amusement and smiled along with him.

In a very few minutes they were eating Steve's delicious supper, in no way spoiled by Barbara's nap. They sat together at Barbara's table, laughing and chatting like old friends. Barbara dug into the delicious meal a little enviously, wishing she could cook as well as Steve. The conversation was general and certainly not provocative, yet there was an undercurrent of sexual tension that both were aware of. Oh, yes, she thought. We're going to have an affair, and we both know it. She found the knowledge as exciting as she had found anything, ever. Steve was as attracted to her as she was to him, and thank God, he would be adult enough to admit it without trying to couch his emotion in a lot of romantic nonsense. And with the way they both felt about marriage, a serious affair was as far as either of them would be willing to take their relationship. It was perfect! So when would the affair commence? Tonight? Probably not. In spite of her nap Barbara was still tired, and the wine she was drinking was making her drowsy. Besides, the beeper could go off at any time. No, as excited as she was at the thought of Steve making love to her, the timing would be better later.

Steve carried his plate into the kitchen and put it in the dishwasher. Barbara followed him, loading the machine with soap and pushing the ON button. At that moment the telephone rang, but fortunately the problem was handled with just a prescription. She made her way back into the living room and flopped down beside Steve, rising almost immediately with a yelp of pain. "Ow! That brush hurt!"

Steve reached down into the cushion and retrieved the offending brush, a plastic one with very firm bristles. "Oh, no!" Barbara exclaimed, running her hands through her damp, tangled hair. It was almost dry, but it had dried in fierce, wild disarray. "Why didn't you tell me? Now I'll have the devil of a time getting those tangles out!" Impatiently she jerked the brush through the side of her hair, wincing when the worst of her fears were realized.

"Sorry," Steve said cheerfully. "I didn't realize that it would be such a mess." He took the brush from her hand and motioned to the carpet by his feet. "Sit down there and I'll get them out for you."

Barbara started to protest, but admitted that he could do no worse than she. Obediently she sat at his feet and tensed herself for the rough session that would be required to remove the tangles. Steve took the end of her swath of hair and brushed gently, skillfully working out the snarls and tangles. When the ends were smooth, he moved further up the hair, repeating the process ever so gently. Barbara was becoming even drowsier, lulled by the silence and the mesmerizing sensation of Steve gently stroking the brush through her hair, over and over. Slowly he worked up until he was brushing out the entire length of her hair. Firm, even strokes tingled Barbara's scalp and sent sleepy tremors of delight down her spine. The feel of the brush was soothing, and Barbara was almost hypnotized by the sensuous, rhythmic repetition. Steve let the hand without the brush fall lower and rub her neck until he could feel the tense muscles relax under his fingers. Barbara let her head roll forward, allowing Steve access to her shoulders, which he then massaged until they, too, were relaxed. Then, before Barbara had time to protest, he set the brush down and pulled her to her feet.

"If I stay any longer I'm going to start something you're too tired to finish," he murmured against her parted lips. He reached down and drank of her lips hungrily, savoring the taste of her mouth. She pressed herself closer to him and looped her arms around his neck, swaying a little. Smiling, Steve disengaged her arms and took her by the hand and led her to her bedroom, his eyes widening as he saw the messy but opulent boudoir that he instinctively knew that she had never shared with a man. Gently he sat her down on the bed and took off her outer clothes, drawing back the covers and slipping her inside clad only in her underwear.

Barbara was aware that he had taken her to her room and was putting her to bed, but she was too tired to care. With a murmured "Thank you," she smiled up at him blindingly and then was asleep.

Steve reached down and kissed her cheek. "I wonder how soon you'll be ready for me," he whispered as he gazed thoughtfully at the beautiful sleeping woman.

Barbara woke to the sound of the ringing telephone. She reached over and picked up the receiver, noting with pleasure the way the sun dappled the sheets and comforter. She had slept later than she had intended. "Dr. Weimer here," she said crisply.

"Good morning," a familiar voice drawled. "Pleasant dreams?"

"Steve!" Barbara sat up abruptly, the covers falling away from her body to expose her almost-naked form. Dimly she remembered Steve brushing out her tangled hair and putting her to bed. Pleasant embarrassment flooded her as she realized the intimate implications of his act.

"Did I wake you?" Steve asked innocently.

"Yes, but that's all right," Barbara said quickly. "What can I do for you this morning?"

"I'm spending the day with you," Steve said cheerfully. "We'll take a picnic lunch to Galveston and spend the day at the beach."

"I can't do that," Barbara said slowly. "I have the beeper, remember?"

66

"Sorry, I'd forgotten," Steve replied. "So do you have to spend the day cooped up at your place? I can bring some tacos for breakfast. . . ."

"Steve, it will be just like the other night," Barbara protested as she shook her hair out of her eyes. "I'll be on the telephone or at the hospital for most of the day. In fact, I have to get up and go make rounds now. Maybe we'd better make it for later."

"Sure," Steve said agreeably. "Be seeing you."

Unreasonably disappointed, Barbara dropped the receiver a little harder than she had to and stomped to the bathroom. Damn! Why did she have to work, today of all days? Didn't she ever deserve to have some fun? She took a quick shower and threw on a pair of designer jeans and a purple smock top, and was soon headed for the hospital.

Rounds took her twice as long as usual, since she had to see Max's patients as well as her own, and it was quite late in the morning when she had finished. She pulled her ponytail out and left the hospital, walking slowly back to her car as she kicked a Coke can down the sidewalk. Hooray, she thought dispiritedly. It's almost noon, and all I have to look forward to for the rest of the day is answering the telephone and probably making one or two more trips down to the hospital.

A hand enclosing her elbow made her whirl in fear, ready to fight for her safety. When she saw that her assailant was Steve, she sagged in relief. "Damn it, Steve! You're making a career out of scaring me to death!"

"Sorry," Steve said unrepentantly. He steered her away from the doctors' parking lot to a public lot a few feet farther away.

"What do you want now?" Barbara snapped, still not over her fright.

"I'm going to spend the day with you," Steve said firmly. "We can't go on a picnic at the beach, but there's no reason that you have to spend the day sitting on your couch waiting for the telephone to ring." His grip on her arm was not bruising, but firm enough so that Barbara could not get away.

67

"Steve, it will be just like the other night," she protested. "I'll spend half my time on the telephone!"

"So?" Steve replied. "You can spend half your time on the phone, and the other half with me." He located his car and unlocked the passenger door, pushing Barbara inside gently. "Now, what are the ground rules for going out with the beeper?"

"You're crazy." Barbara sighed as she opened her purse. Fishing around, she unearthed a roll of quarters and nodded. "I have enough quarters to last most, if not all, of the afternoon, so we don't need to get any of those. I have to stay close to a telephone, that's all. Really, Steve, wouldn't you rather—"

Steve silenced her with a hard kiss, brief but spine tingling. "Does that answer your question?" he asked harshly, his breathing ragged.

Barbara nodded, stunned from the impact of his kiss. Steve pulled out of the parking lot and headed away from the medical complex, driving toward the affluent suburbs. Barbara leaned her head back on the headrest and studied her companion. Physically appealing? Definitely. But Steve Sullivan was something more. He's arrogant, she thought, remembering the way he had shanghaied her last week in the parking lot and again today in front of the hospital. He wants his own way. But he couldn't have been any nicer last night, she reminded herself as she remembered the way he had cooked her supper when she was too tired to look at him straight. Barbara shook her head. He's an enigma, she thought. I'll never figure him out!

Steve pulled into the parking lot of the largest shopping mall in Houston. "We're going shopping?" Barbara asked, secretly delighted. The Galleria was more than just a shopping mall. It was three stories tall, boasted a hotel, a number of nightclubs, a health club complete with jogging path on the roof, and a number of fine restaurants. It was said that many visitors to Houston never went beyond the Galleria. "I haven't been here in ages!" Barbara volunteered excitedly as she hopped from the car.

They entered through the large swinging doors of the super-mall just as Barbara's beeper went off. Steve spotted a phone booth and Barbara fished out her roll of quarters. It was Netta Morris again with another list of complaints. Barbara stuck her finger in her ear to shut out the noise of the mall and convinced Netta that a hospital visit for a mild cold was not really neces-sary. Shaking her head, Barbara called the pharmacy for a mild decongestant and finally was able to return to Steve, who was sitting on a bench watching a couple of buxom teen-age girls bounce by. "You better watch it," she whispered in Steve's ear. "You're going to get eyestrain that way."

"Believe me, it would be worth it!" Steve quipped. Barbara laughed as she reached out and took Steve's hand.

"You sure took a long time with that call," Steve said as they strolled down the crowded mall. "Anything serious?"

"Yes and no," Barbara said. "The actual medical problem was just a cold, but the underlying psychological problems go much further. That was my office hypochondriac."

"Have you eaten anything today?" Steve asked.

"No, and your steak is about to wear off," Barbara admitted.

Steve pointed out a Chinese restaurant that Barbara had never visited. She nodded, and before too long they were seated at a small table and had placed their order. "Tell me about the hypo-chondriac," Steve said as the waiter walked away.

"Actually, she is only one of several that Max and I have," Barbara said as she sipped her water. "They are mostly older women whose children are gone and who have nothing to do. They don't have an interest in life so they turn to their own bodies as a source of attention. Every slight ache or pain gets magnified into something major."

"And they pester you," Steve added shrewdly.

"I hate to use the word 'pester,' " Barbara said, "because the pain is very real to them. But, yes, some days I cringe when I see them coming with their list."

"They bring a list?" Steve asked, incredulous. The waiter

69

brought their meal and Barbara dug gratefully into the moo goo gai pan.

"Sure they do," she said as she swallowed the delicious concoction. "How else are they going to remember it all? And I swear I don't know the solution for it."

"Actually, the solution in some cases could be fairly simple," Steve said thoughtfully as he waded into his shrimp with bacon.

"What, what? Help me!" Barbara teased.

"Seriously, you goof." Steve laughed as he bit into his egg roll. "Those women need another interest in life. A job or volunteer work or something."

Barbara rolled her eyes. "You think it would be that simple?" she scoffed as she sipped the delicate cup of tea.

"For most of them it probably would," Steve replied. "One of my neighbors used to be the worst hypochondriac you ever knew. If she wasn't on the telephone to her doctor at least three times a week, the poor doctor felt rejected. Then Ellen's daughter got a divorce and brought the grandchildren over to stay with Ellen while she went to work. Now the doctor sees the kids sometimes, but he never sees Grandma anymore!"

"You probably have something there," Barbara said slowly. "I'll remember that!" Here I am again, she thought as she realized what was happening. She was discussing one of her problems with Steve, and he had even come up with a possible solution. It was so easy and comfortable to talk to him!

They chatted about various things for the rest of the meal, enjoying the camaraderie and the excitement that was building between them. The magic was flowing, and Barbara shivered as she realized what that mystic feeling meant. Tonight's the night, she told herself excitedly. She looked across the table and smiled slightly, a silent invitation in her eyes. Steve looked back at her, acceptance in his. Tonight *was* the night.

Almost giddy with excitement, they left the restaurant holding hands and swinging their arms together. Barbara's beeper went off again, but the problem was quickly dealt with and they spent

70

nearly an hour poking through the interesting boutiques that filled the mall. Steve threatened to buy her a set of Frankenstein tools in a novelty store, and Barbara tried on a gauzy lace dress imported from Mexico, groaning in disappointment when it proved simply too large. Steve treated her to an ice cream cone and they watched the skaters in the huge ice-rink whirl and glide as they ate their cones.

"I wish I could do that," Barbara said thoughtfully as she savored the last of her crunchy cone.

"Well, why don't we?" Steve asked.

"You're kidding!" Barbara said as she wadded up her napkin. "I've never ice-skated in my life! I'll break my neck!"

"No, you won't," Steve scoffed. "It's easy. Can you roller-skate at all?"

"Of course," Barbara replied. "I'm actually quite good at it."

"Well, this is no different. Just keep your ankles a little tighter."

Barbara eyed the skaters thoughtfully. It really looked like fun. Throwing her napkin into the trash, she grabbed Steve's hand and ran him toward the entrance to the rink. "Okay, you're on."

Steve grinned sheepishly. "I really didn't think you'd do it." He paid their admission, then they selected skates and strapped them on. Gingerly Barbara stood up. On the thick carpet of the dressing room the heavy skates were surprisingly easy to walk on. Using her hands to balance her weight, she walked to the rink entrance and tentatively slid out onto the ice. Immediately her ankles started to buckle. She instinctively tightened her calf and ankle muscles and, using the same motions that she would have on a roller rink, made her way around the ice, wobbling a little but slowly becoming surer in her motions.

As she came up on the entrance to the dressing room, she spotted Steve waiting by the entrance, a peculiarly tense expression on his face. "Come on!" Barbara called. "It's great!"

With a jerky motion Steve propelled himself out onto the ice and almost before Barbara could blink had fallen down, his long legs sliding out from him with astonishing speed. Barbara skated to him as quickly as she could and tried to haul him back onto his feet, but slipped and landed on top of him instead. Steve rolled away from Barbara and stood up shakily. This time he managed to skate about ten feet before his legs flew out from under him again. Barbara slowly rose to her feet and shoved her fist in front of her face to keep from laughing out loud. This was the man who had made it all sound so easy!

Gritting his teeth, Steve stood up and tried again. By the time he had made it around the rink once, he was considerably more secure on the skates, but he could not match the graceful gliding motion that Barbara was finding so natural. Gasping for breath, he leaned against the rail and glared at her. "You've done this before!" he accused her indignantly.

"Nope. Never," Barbara denied, laughing out loud at Steve's ineptness. He glowered back, his masculine ego wounded. "Look, would it help if I admitted that I'm a whiz on roller skates?" she asked. "Are you?"

"No," Steve admitted glumly. "I never took the time to learn."

"Then quit pouting and skate with me!" Barbara taunted impudently as she took off for another spin around the ice.

They skated for half an hour, Steve quickly improving his skill on the ice. Barbara tried to duplicate her speed on roller skates, but admitted to herself that it would take a lot of practice before she could do that. They were leaning against the rail, watching a pair of figure skaters practice, when Barbara's beeper went off.

"Got to go call," Barbara said with a sigh as she patted the little nuisance strapped to her belt. She skated toward the dressing room and clomped clumsily to the telephone.

Dave Barclay's voice sounded excited on the telephone. "Janet's pains are six minutes apart and coming hard. Should we go on down?"

"Definitely," Barbara replied, reaching down to untie her

skate. "I'll be along in a few minutes. Remember, Dave, help her with her breathing."

"Sure thing," Dave replied. "See you in a little while."

Barbara sat down on the bench and unlaced her skates. Usually she waited for a call from labor and delivery before she went in, but in the heavy Saturday traffic and as far as they were from the hospital, she might as well start over now. Steve wandered in and sat down beside her. "Had enough already?" he asked in surprise.

"No," Barbara admitted with a rueful smile. "I have to go back to the hospital and deliver a baby."

"That's all right," Steve said as he sat down and took off his skates. Barbara shot him a puzzled look. "I was tired of having a mere woman show me up out there," he said with great dignity, sniffing haughtily as Barbara laughed out loud.

"I can see the crown now, Janet. You're doing great. Now, take a deep breath and bear down. Hard. That's super. Now rest until the next contraction."

Janet's face was drenched in sweat and contorted in concentration. Dave stood beside her, holding her hand and murmuring encouraging words in her ear. These young couples had grit! Barbara was frequently amazed at the strength and love she saw displayed in the delivery room. Even though she had delivered a good number of babies by now, she still marveled at the power of the human spirit and the shared joy of bringing a life into the world. And she got to share that joy every time.

"One more time, Janet," Barbara said as she checked the position of the infant. Janet pushed for all she was worth. The tiny head was nearly out! Barbara guided the little head around. "A gentle push this time, Janet," she said. Janet obeyed and the tiny, slippery baby made its entrance. "You've got a boy!" she said.

"A boy! Let me see him!" Janet demanded. Barbara obediently

73

held up the tiny infant as she drained his nose with a syringe. Almost immediately he set up a lusty howl.

Barbara handed the baby to the nurse. "What's his name?" Barbara asked as she tended to Janet.

"David Preston Barclay, the Third," Janet replied proudly.

"Named after his old man, hmm?" Barbara asked as she watched the couple absorbed by the sight of the squirming infant who was theirs. Barbara bade the couple good-bye and promised to see both mother and son early in the morning. She entered the women's dressing room and removed her greens, then walked to the doctor's lounge for a cup of coffee before she headed for home.

But before she had even entered the lounge, she spotted the familiar brown head, bent over another thriller. "Steve! It's been hours! Why haven't you gone on home?" She had thought that their day was over, but he had waited for her instead. She was delighted and it showed in the dazzling smile she graced Steve with. So Janet Barclay's baby had not changed the now almost certain climax to this day. She and Steve would be lovers before the night was out and that thought filled Barbara with delicious anticipation.

"I don't give up that easily," Steve said lightly as he took her elbow. "What's this? Tears again?"

"Not exactly," Barbara said. "It's just such a joy to deliver a baby that I . . ." She trailed off uncertainly.

"Softie!" Steve taunted gently. "Care to eat at my place tonight?" he asked with deceptive casualness.

"I'd love to," Barbara stammered, desperately trying to match his casual tone and failing miserably. Steve smiled a little at her nervousness.

Steve drove them to a sprawling ranch house in one of the newer subdivisions off Westheimer. Barbara openly admired the huge, carefully casual but spotlessly neat home and furnishings, chosen to harmonize and please but not to overpower. Steve invited her to show herself around while he cooked their supper.

74

Barbara started to protest but a suspicious rumbling in her stomach reminded her that it was time for an evening meal. As Steve took himself off to the kitchen, Barbara nosed around the spacious home, counting four bedrooms and a master suite that opened onto a small swimming pool. Steve's suite was decorated with stunning effectiveness in cobalt-blue and white, and managed to be completely comfortable and totally masculine at the same time. Barbara wandered back into what appeared to be a private den that was right off the dining room. It was decorated in earth tones and sported a large color television. But the room was dominated by a huge white fur rug in the middle of the floor in front of the fireplace. Barbara knelt down and stroked it hesitantly at first, then with growing boldness as her fingers looped through the sensuously soft fur. That would be a wonderful place to make love!

Barbara laughed and skipped back to the kitchen. "I didn't know you were a frustrated game hunter."

"Oh, you noticed the rug," Steve said as he shredded the lettuce for a salad. "I'll have you know that thing is the most comfortable rug that I have ever watched TV on," he said with mock sternness.

"Good for other things, too, I guess," Barbara said, suddenly horribly jealous. How many women had shared Steve's rug with him before her? And how many would after her?

Steve looked at her shrewdly. "I wouldn't know. I haven't had it long," he volunteered. Barbara looked at him skeptically. "No, I mean that. Look, Barbara, I'm not a saint, but I'm a hell of a lot more discriminating than you must think."

"Sorry," Barbara whispered. "It's just that this is new to me. I hear so much . . ."

Steve placed a gentle finger on her lips. "I'm flattered that you think enough of me to be jealous," he said as he replaced his finger with his mouth.

It started as a gentle kiss, but before Barbara could stop herself she had melted into Steve's embrace and he was clinging to her

75

mindlessly. They stood locked together in a timeless whirl of emotion, wiping all the doubts and jealousy from Barbara's mind. She had no need to be jealous of Steve. He wanted to become her lover, and she wanted to become his. She had nothing to worry about. She reached out and slowly undid the top buttons of his shirt, reaching in to run her fingers through the thick light-brown hair that covered his lean chest. Steve gasped at the sensations that her nimble fingers were creating. He ran his fingers through her thick hair and arched his lower body against hers briefly, causing Barbara to melt against him in breathless longing, her body aching to complete their intimacy. Steve ran his hands down her hips, then gently pushed her away. "If we keep on with this, you won't get any supper." He stepped away from her reluctantly.

Still caught up in her fiery emotions, Barbara started to protest, then her stomach growled again and she realized that she was frightfully hungry. Steve turned back to the stove and removed a delicious-looking chicken and a casserole of vegetables. "How did you cook those so quickly?" Barbara asked in astonishment.

"Ever heard of a timer?" Steve asked dryly. Barbara made iced tea and listened while Steve told her all about the joys of learning to cook after his divorce. She admitted that she was not as good a cook as she would like to be, but said in self-defense that she intended to learn soon. Together they sat down to Steve's excellent meal.

The food was delicious, but Barbara would have been just as pleased with a bologna sandwich. It was the company that made tonight so special. Delicious anticipation spiced their conversation and movements. Each was exquisitely sensitive to every nuance, stoking the small flame that would explode into an inferno before the night was over. They finished their meal and Steve reached out and grasped Barbara's palm and nibbled it lightly. "I have a cake for dessert," he murmured as his sensitive mouth sent sensual chills up Barbara's arm.

"Th-that's okay," Barbara stammered. "I'll pass."

Steve grinned wickedly. "I guess you get me for dessert, then," he murmured as he took her into his arms.

"We can eat it later," Barbara volunteered as Steve grasped her by the shoulders and pulled her to her feet. He pulled her to him and captured her willing mouth with his, drowning her in his sensual embrace. Barbara slid her hands around his waist and pulled his body against hers, moaning with delight at the evidence of his desire for her.

Steve reluctantly broke the embrace. "Would you like to make love on the rug?" he asked hoarsely.

Entranced, Barbara nodded. Steve picked her up and carried her to his fur rug. He put her down and without speaking his hands went to the smock top and pulled it over her head. He then reached down and thumbed her nipples, smiling in satisfaction as they hardened beneath the silky bra. Barbara reached out and unbuttoned Steve's shirt and slid it across his shoulders, shivering as she realized just how accurately she had pictured the upper part of his sensual body. Hungrily she ran her fingers around his waist and drew him closer to her, gasping with pleasure as Steve deftly removed her bra and the hair on his chest scraped her sensitive breasts. He reached down and unsnapped her jeans and pulled them off, then hooked his thumbs into her panties and pulled them down her legs. Firmly capturing her mouth with his, Steve lowered Barbara onto the rug.

The soft fur tickled Barbara's back and legs, and she rolled over so that she could feel its sensuous caress on her breasts and stomach. Steve reached down and grasped the small of her waist in his hands, kneading the soft flesh of her back. "Ooh, that feels good!" Barbara exclaimed as the tense muscles in her waist and back relaxed under Steve's ministrations. He slid his hands up past her shoulder blades to her shoulders, finding the tight knotted muscles in her neck and easing the tension out of those, too, as Barbara whimpered with pleasure. His hands slid back down to her waist and then lower, caressing her buttocks lovingly as

Barbara gasped at his daring. Barbara melted into the rug, perfectly willing for Steve to caress her all night, and she jumped with surprise when he reached out and swatted her bottom playfully.

"Turn over," he demanded. "I want to see the rest of you."

Barbara complied willingly. She wound her slender arms around Steve's hard waist, pulling his body against hers and feeling his aroused masculinity against her hips. Steve bestowed a trail of kisses down her throat to her bare breasts, taking one swelling nipple into his mouth and suckling it gently. The delicious excitement spread through Barbara's chest and stomach and down to the center of her femininity. Her hands slid down his hips. She reached out and unzipped Steve's jeans, but they stubbornly refused to slide down his legs.

Impatiently Steve reached down and tugged them off and threw them across the room; then he pushed Barbara back into the soft pelt and surveyed her body with caressing eyes. "You are so beautiful," he murmured as he drank in her naked form.

"I knew you would be beautiful," Barbara volunteered as she reached over and slipped the briefs from Steve's body. He was as gorgeous as she had imagined, and she ran her hands down his hips greedily. "I could tell that first day in the hospital when I touched you."

Steve reached out and pulled her to him. "My God, I've dreamed of doing this ever since I saw you from the skyscraper," he murmured. He reached down and covered her mouth and her face with kisses, and lowered his taut body onto hers. He parted her legs with his and captured Barbara completely.

Barbara arched upward to meet Steve's possession and gasped at the sensations he was arousing in her. Quickly, quickly, the excitement built, and Barbara tensed. Steve moaned and arched his back, and together they plunged into shared ecstasy. Barbara gripped Steve's hips as pleasure washed over her, holding him to her to savor the wane of a delight that ended too quickly.

Steve reached out and caressed Barbara's face gently. "We should have taken our time," he said ruefully.

"That's all right. I-I'm fine," Barbara stammered.

"I know that," Steve answered, laughing. He pulled her on top of him. "But I want to make it better for you this time. . . . What was that?"

Barbara sat up and put her head in her hands. "The beeper," she said disgustedly, her hair falling around her.

"I don't believe it," Steve muttered. Suddenly his eyes danced with mischief. "Go make your call, and if it's Netta, tell her I'll send her a whole notepad if she'll just leave you alone for tonight."

Grinning, her humor restored, Barbara crawled off the rug and walked across the floor to the telephone. Steve drank in the beauty of her nakedness as she placed her call, waiting eagerly for her to return to his arms. Barbara dialed her service and was given her message. "Oh, hell!" she said out loud as she called the emergency room. The clerk on duty gave Barbara what little information she had about an injury to one of Max's patients. Although the clerk was not sure of the details, Barbara knew that there was no way to weasel out of this one.

Thoroughly put out, she slammed down the receiver and reached for her panties and pulled them back on. "I've got to go back to the hospital," she snapped. "I guess the evening's shot." Angry frustration welled up inside of her as she fumbled with her bra. Why, tonight of all nights? Just when she and Steve had made such beautiful love, just when they were about to make love again . . .

"Hey, maybe it's not the end of the evening," Steve said reasonably as he put his clothes on. Firmly controlling his own frustration, he took her in his arms and kissed her, feeling her tender breasts against his chest. "I'll take you down there and you can dispense with whatever, and then we come back here for the rest of dessert. It isn't that late, you know."

"You're right," Barbara said. In their haste they had made love at an almost indecently early hour. "I'll hurry."

She pulled on the rest of her clothes with lightning speed, and Steve drove her to the hospital as fast as he dared on the busy city streets. "It's some kind of injury in emergency," Barbara volunteered as they jumped out of the car. "One of Max's patients was in a bar fight and hadn't arrived at the hospital when they called. The clerk wasn't sure how badly he was hurt."

"I'm Dr. Weimer," she volunteered as she strode up to the desk. "Has the patient arrived yet?"

"Yeah," the clerk said disgustedly as she thumbed toward the trauma room. "The so-and-so's in there."

"May I come along?" Steve asked at her elbow. "I'd like to see you work."

"I think it would be all right," Barbara said as she turned toward the trauma room. Her body was limp from their lovemaking, and all she wanted was to return to Steve's warm embrace. Don't worry—you'll be back in Steve's arms before you know it, she promised herself as they entered the trauma room.

A large, middle-aged man lay on the table, moaning loudly in pain. "You gotta help me, Doc!" he complained, turning bloodshot eyes on Steve. "I'm in such turrible agony!" His breath smelled of cheap liquor.

"I'm the doc," Barbara said briskly as she washed her hands. "Now, what happened?"

"Oh, Doc, I hurt so bad! That son of a bitch, he shot me, and it hurts so bad! You gotta help me!"

"I'm going to do just that," Barbara said soothingly as she pulled back the sheet. The man had suffered a bullet wound to the upper part of his calf. Barbara reached down and lifted the injured leg slightly.

"Oww!" the man cried, breathing more liquor fumes all over Barbara. "Damn it, Doc, that leg hurts!"

Barbara bit back a sarcastic reply. "I have to examine your leg," she said firmly. "Just lie still and it won't take long." She

80

examined the front of the wound and then felt the bones. The man screamed and moaned and swore with every move she made, and Barbara fought back the urge to tell him to shut up. The injury was not serious, with no damage to the bones, but there was no exit wound, which meant that the bullet was still inside.

Straightening up, Barbara replaced the sheet over the lower portion of the man's body. "I'm afraid the bullet is still in there. I'm going to have to take it out."

"Oh, you can't do that! It'll hurt too much!" the man wailed.

"Believe me, it will hurt a lot worse if I leave it in!" Barbara snapped.

"How long?" Steve whispered into Barbara's ear.

She looked at him with frustration clearly mirrored in her face. "Two hours at least. Maybe longer."

Steve nodded. "I'll wait," he said firmly.

Steve is something else, Barbara thought as she bent back over her patient to take another look at his leg. Suddenly the man turned his head to the open doorway and raised himself up on his elbows, pushing Barbara out of his line of vision. Lifting a shaky hand, he pointed to the stretcher that was rolling by the door. "There he is!" he screamed as he struggled to pull himself up. "There goes the son of a bitch who shot me!"

Barbara quickly looked at the man on the stretcher being pushed by the door, accompanied by two policemen. He was small and mean-looking and appeared to be no more than a kid.

She immediately turned her attention back to her patient, who was now being restrained by Steve from jumping off the table. The older man swore violently, twisting in Steve's hold. Barbara, terrified but not allowing her terror to show on her face, knew that Steve needed help.

She ran to the open door. "Officer, come quickly," she yelled at the backs of the policemen following the stretcher down the long corridor. One of them turned and saw Barbara motioning toward the room she had just stepped out of. He quickly made his way to her and brushed past her into the room. On seeing the struggle between the two men, he forcefully wedged himself between them and managed to subdue the injured man by handcuffing him and laying him back down on the table. The officer turned to Barbara. "Are you all right, Doctor?"

Barbara nodded, as the policeman glanced at Steve, who reassured him with a slightly cocky grin that he was none the worse for the skirmish.

Barbara impatiently ran her hand through her hair. "Well, officer, if that will be all, I'd appreciate it if you'd remove the handcuffs so I can get my patient up to surgery," Barbara stated, smiling faintly.

"Sure thing, Doctor," he responded, turning to the man on the table and taking the handcuffs from his wrists. "Well, there is just one thing," he said, as he turned back to face Barbara. "That punk has a stab wound that needs to be seen to, and I thought since you were already here and all . . ."

"Of course, officer, I'll see him," Barbara said wearily as he walked out the door.

She looked at Steve, her dismay plainly written across her face. "I'll be here all night," she said disgustedly. Visions of Steve's sensuous body danced before her eyes, and she was sorely tempted to inflict further injury on both of her patients just to get even. "Tomorrow?" she asked hopefully.

Steve's shoulders sagged. "I have Scooter all day," he said softly. Seeing the defeat in Barbara's eyes, his own lit up wickedly. "Just think," he offered, his eyes glinting, "next weekend you won't have the beeper!" And before Barbara could protest he pushed her into an empty treatment room and kissed her until she was moaning; then he left her to her work.

It was dawn before Barbara left the hospital. Dragging her weary body to her car, she sighed in frustration as she imagined where she would have been right now if the beeper had not gone off. She would have been locked in Steve's arms, maybe making love to him for the third or fourth time. Damn! Her fist hit the steering wheel. Then a disturbing thought crossed her mind. Why on earth did making love to Steve again matter so much to her? He was just a man. They were only having an affair. It was not the romance of the century. For goodness' sakes, it was not that big a deal. Or was it?

CHAPTER FIVE

"Well, Dr. Weimer, how did I check out this time?" Phil Harris asked as he buttoned his shirt. He was a good-looking, successful businessman in his early forties, sporting a little paunch but otherwise in excellent health.

"You're one of the few who probably doesn't even need to be in here," she added with a grin.

"I know that," Phil answered brightly. "I just come to eye the doctor."

"Sure," Barbara scoffed. "You know that you don't have eyes for anyone but Jeannie. How's the family, by the way?"

"Just great," Phil continued as he buttoned his expensive cuff links. "Jeannie's gone back to school after twenty years, can you believe it? And Marilyn's getting pretty serious about this new boy she's dating."

Isn't she, though, thought Barbara to herself.

"Mike is finishing his senior year and playing quarterback for his team this fall. First string."

"And you're just as proud as you can be," Barbara added aloud this time.

"You bet!" Phil said.

"Okay, Phil, I couldn't be more pleased on the whole with your health. But do try to take off about ten pounds. You'll be back down to your ideal weight then."

"Sure thing, Dr. Weimer. Be seeing you."

There goes a man who has everything, Barbara thought as she finished with his chart and left it with Sylvia. A happy family life, a successful business, good kids. She pushed her hair, which had come loose from her ponytail, behind her ear and returned to her office. As she passed Max's office door, she glanced over to see him pacing the floor furiously with the telephone in one hand and a cigarette in the other.

"No, Eileen, I can't possibly take the children this weekend. I have the beeper and—" He broke off and listened to a spate of angry words coming over the wire. "No, I can't possibly ask her. She had the beeper last weekend and—Yes, I realize that you have to live your own life and need to get away. . . . Yes, I want you to find someone else and get married again. . . . All right, I'll ask her." Max laid the receiver down on his desk and turned toward the door. When he saw that Barbara had been listening, his face turned a bright shade of red and he shrugged helplessly. "Eileen wants to go away for the weekend," he stammered. "I wonder if—"

"If I can take the beeper," Barbara finished slowly. A slow, building anger burned through Barbara. Normally she would have been put out, but she would have gone ahead and taken the beeper. But not this weekend. No way! She and Steve had been simply too busy to do more than meet for coffee on Monday, and they had some unfinished business that Barbara was not about to have interrupted by the beeper again. She shook her head. "No, Max. Not this weekend."

Max picked up the telephone. "She can't take it this weekend," he said. "Yes, I asked her. She has things to do. I don't know what. It's none of my business." Max listened for a moment, then turned to Barbara hesitantly. "She wants to speak to you."

"Are you sure you want that?" Barbara asked him slowly. "I won't pull any punches with her."

"I won't get any peace if you don't," Max admitted.

Reluctantly Barbara picked up the receiver. "Dr. Weimer here."

"Oh, Barbara, could you please take the beeper so that Max can take the kids? I have the chance to go on the most marvelous weekend, and I need to relax so desperately," Eileen whined into the telephone.

"So do I," Barbara said evenly. "You should have planned your trip for last weekend when Max had the kids."

"I just couldn't," Eileen said petulantly. "Couldn't you please take the beeper?"

"No way," Barbara said firmly. "Hire a baby-sitter." There was an audible gasp on the other end of the line. "Good-bye, Eileen." Very gently Barbara hung up the telephone and turned to Max. "There. You see how easy it is?"

"I know, I know," Max muttered as he shuffled his list of calls to be made. "But it doesn't work that way for me."

"When you get fed up enough it will," Barbara predicted cheerfully as she returned to her own office. Her own list of calls was relatively short, and before long she was swinging out the doors and into her car, free from the beeper and her practice for two blessed days. Steve had gone out of town on business, but she was due to pick him up at the airport first thing in the morning, and the rest of the weekend would be theirs.

Barbara spent her evening preparing herself for the weekend to come. She washed her hair and conditioned it, and painted her fingernails and her toenails a bright shade of pink. After her nails dried, she did her long-neglected sit-ups and found an old jar of a facial mudpack that she had forgotten she had. Standing at the mirror, she laughed at herself as she stroked the ugly mixture onto her face. "All this isn't going to make one whit of difference in the way you look, and you know it. You just think it will." Why is this weekend so important to me? she wondered for the hundredth time since last Saturday. She slapped on the last of the mudpack and looked at herself in the mirror, her bright blue eyes staring out of the mud like two Christmas stars. I'm just like a girl going to her first prom, she thought, remembering the care with which she had bought herself a new dress, for once worried about her clothes. This isn't me, I don't act like this, she said over and over. But she was acting like this. And she realized that she

86

was powerless to change either her feelings or her behavior. Am I that anxious to be with a man? she wondered as she returned to the living room for another round of sit-ups. Is all the folklore about deprived divorcées true? But she hadn't felt especially deprived until she met Steve.

Barbara jumped as the telephone rang. Oh, she hoped it was Steve! She answered the telephone and heard her mother's clear voice on the other end, eagerly asking how her favorite daughter was doing. Delighted to hear her mother's voice, Barbara sat down cross-legged on the floor and talked to her mother for the better part of an hour. Although her parents lived in the nearby town of Rosenberg, sometimes three or four weeks went by when Barbara was too busy to go by and see them, and the telephone was a handy way of staying in touch. Barbara casually mentioned that she had met someone, and she could have sworn that Mrs. Weimer was jumping up and down for joy in the middle of her kitchen floor. It was her mother's dearest wish to see Barbara married again, and although Barbara had tried to let her mother know how she felt about another marriage, Mrs. Weimer refused to take the hint.

You know, I shouldn't have said anything, Barbara thought later as she hung up the telephone. Her mother would have her married off by morning! Barbara thought about her parents as she washed the mudpack off her face, and she knew for certain that they would be hurt when they found out what kind of relationship she and Steve were having. Barbara sighed and returned to the living room, sitting on the sofa and cradling a throw pillow in her lap. How would her affair affect her parents? Oh, they would try to understand, but they would be hurt.

Hell, Barbara thought as she realized what the affair would mean. She and Steve would be discreet, of course, but in the long run her parents would know. Barbara lay back on the sofa and closed her eyes. How did she feel about that? She just didn't know. Was the drawback to an affair with Steve enough to stop her?

"No," she said out loud, very firmly. She was not about to quit Steve now, not when happiness with him was virtually in her grasp. As for her parents, she sincerely hoped that they would forgive her and, maybe, understand just a little.

Barbara watched the jet taxi down the runway and stop beside the caterpillarlike ramp that led directly into the airport terminal. She searched the crowd as the passengers spilled into the waiting room and finally spotted that brown head of hair, its sun-streaking even more evident than it had been when Steve left. Barbara knew that he had gone to check on a job in central Mexico, and from his sunburned nose she suspected that he had spent much of his time outdoors. She ran to him through the crowd and he whisked her off her feet, swinging her around and kissing her soundly. "Miss me?" he asked lightly.

"You bet!" Barbara replied as she reached up and kissed the tip of his nose. "So how were things down there?"

"Better than I expected," Steve said as he shouldered his flight bag. They set off toward the baggage claim area with Barbara holding Steve's arm lightly. He selected two battered suitcases from the snake-shaped conveyor belt and they headed for the parking lot, stowing Steve's luggage in the trunk of the Corvette. Steve shoved a box of drug samples out of the passenger seat and slid in beside Barbara. "I take it that you're the chauffeur today," he said as Barbara exited the parking lot.

"Where to?" she asked gaily.

"Back to my place for a bath and change, then anywhere your heart desires," Steve replied.

Barbara looked up at the gathering clouds in the sky. "I thought we'd have a picnic on the beach," she said slowly. She bit her lip in thought. It didn't really matter what they did today. They would be together and minus the distraction of the beeper. But maybe it did matter to Steve. "What would you like to do?" she asked.

"Grocery shopping." Barbara looked at Steve in surprise.

"Checkers. Paint the kitchen. Frankly, Barbara, as long as we do it together, it doesn't really matter what we do."

Barbara reached out and squeezed his hand. "I feel that way, too," she volunteered, warmed by his desire to be with her.

Steve showered and shaved in record time while Barbara made a hamper of sandwiches and other picnic treats. She added a bottle of chilled wine from Steve's refrigerator for good measure, and a huge bag of chips to satisfy her desire for crunchy food. She was waiting in the living room when Steve, freshly showered and smelling of aftershave, appeared clad in a denim shirt and faded jeans. He pulled her up off the couch and wrapped his arms around her, kissing her hungrily. Barbara reached around his waist and hugged him to her. "My God, I missed you," she murmured when Steve released her lips.

"I almost came back last night," Steve admitted. "If I had been able to get a flight, I would have."

"It's a good thing you didn't." Barbara giggled. "You would have caught me with my mudpack."

"Yes, you're right," Steve said as he carried the hamper to the car. "No sense in destroying any romantic illusions," he laughed. "At least until we have to."

What does he mean by that? Barbara wondered. In the type of relationship they were contemplating, there would be no need for romantic illusions ever to be destroyed. She started to ask Steve what he'd meant, but he had placed the hamper in the Corvette and opened her door. "I'll let you drive, since the Jag is sitting on empty."

"Fair enough," Barbara agreed.

The air was sultry but cool enough for comfort, and the sky was cloudy but not depressingly so. Barbara drove aimlessly for a few minutes, then changed lanes with purpose and took a cloverleaf onto another freeway. "I've haven't been to San Jacinto State Park or seen the battleship *Texas* in years," she said suddenly.

"I'll bet it's been a good ten years since I've been," Steve mused. "I gather that's where we're going?"

"Is that all right?" Barbara asked eagerly.

Steve nodded. In a little while they were outside Houston and driving up the long straight drive into the park. Barbara parked her car and gazed up at the tall, pointed monument. "It's because of this battleground that we're speaking English and not Spanish at the moment," she mused. "This is where the Texans won the War of Independence from Mexico."

"With that hair of yours, you would have made a lousy Mexican," Steve teased as he picked up a strand of the platinum tresses.

"Actually, it's really black," Barbara quipped. "I bleach it."

Steve laughed out loud. "Sorry. There is no way that you could achieve this artificially," he said as he rubbed a small strand between his thumb and forefinger. "Your German ancestry, I presume?"

"I'm German and Dutch, mostly," Barbara admitted. "They settled most of south and central Texas at the time of and right after the Civil War."

"Did your ancestors keep alive the language and the traditions of the old country?"

Barbara nodded. "I'm actually the first generation not to speak German," she admitted. "Opa and Oma both had very pronounced accents."

"You called them 'Grandpa' and 'Grandma' in German?" he asked.

Barbara nodded. "I wish now that I had learned the language." She started her car and drove toward the battleship. "Where were your people from?" she asked.

"They moved down here from a New York tenement in the twenties. Houston was a boomtown even then, and Grandpa and Grandma worked hard and made good. My father had a weakness for liquor and ladies, so they calmly bypassed him and left their inheritance to me."

"Was he furious?" Barbara asked as she parked her car as close to the battleship as she could.

"Yes, and he still is, most of the time. When he sobers up, he admits that they had the right idea." Although Steve's manner was offhand, Barbara detected a certain amount of pain in the words.

"Do you resent your father?" she asked.

"No, I feel sorry for him," Steve said softly. "But I made up my mind never to be like him, just letting life drift with me where it will. I make up my mind what I want, and then I get it." Steve got out of the car and locked the door.

Barbara sat quite still for a moment. Deeply disturbed, she turned his statement over in her mind, trying in vain to figure out why it bothered her so. There was certainly nothing wrong in knowing what you wanted out of life and going after it. Wasn't that what she herself had done? So why the unease? She should be admiring Steve for the trait! She thought about his life and the balance that he had achieved, and she realized that he had reached that balance because he had made up his mind to do so. So why was she upset?

Suddenly, the truth dawned. She was afraid! Steve not only had a strong will, his will was in fact much stronger than her own! And this scared her. God, she thought, if we ever do come to a clashing of wills, I'm going to be the loser.

Barbara and Steve spent a delightful two hours touring the interior of the old battleship. They climbed down narrow steps deep into the interior and covered every inch of the beautifully restored vessel. Steve marveled at the low ceilings and narrow bunks in the crew's quarters, lying down on a bunk and laughing at the way his feet hung over the edge. Barbara found the engine room fascinating. Deep within the interior of the ship, it seemed vast after the narrow, cramped spaces in the rest of the vessel. Steve told her a little about the engines that had been in the *Texas*, and Barbara nodded with interest but admitted to herself that she understood very little of what he was saying. They admired the unexpected opulence of the officers' dining rooms, and both were surprised by the quality and quantity of the silver serving pieces. Barbara admitted that she preferred her office to the ship's sick bay, although it was certainly more than adequate, and in its day had probably been the finest.

"So you think you'd rather practice on dry land?" Steve teased her as she poked around the small office.

"Absolutely," Barbara replied. "Can you imagine trying to take out an appendix in a gale-force blow?"

Steve admitted that he could not.

They peeked out portholes and strolled the deck, inspecting with interest the old guns mounted there. Steve held Barbara's hand and she could feel the delicious anticipation building between them again. They would make love again tonight, and she did not have the beeper to call her away. Steve led her to the bridge, where they imagined what it would have been like to steer the *Texas* into battle. Finally they acknowledged the fact that it was well past lunchtime and that their stomachs were both empty. At that moment the first drop of rain hit Barbara's nose, and she looked up to see a very dark cloud that was about to pour down on them. "We'd better make a run for it!" she cried as the second drop hit her nose.

They were too late. By the time they had reached the car they were both soaked. Barbara unlocked the door, but before she could open it, Steve swung her around and pulled her into his arms, locking his lips onto hers and kissing her passionately as the warm rain beat down upon their heads and shoulders. He slid his arms around her, lifting her sodden hair from her neck and drawing her closer to him. Barbara threw her arms around his wet shoulders, feeling every muscle in his arms and back through his clinging shirt. Their kisses and embraces were growing sweeter and sweeter, and Barbara eagerly awaited the culmination of their passion that would come later. Steve drew back and wiped the rain from Barbara's face, kissing her nose and opening the car door. "Get me some lunch, woman," he growled. "I'm hungry."

Barbara pulled the hamper out from behind the seat. "I think we better eat in the car," she said as she set the hamper between them. As she unwrapped her first sandwich, Steve hunched forward and pulled off his soaking shirt, leaving a vast expanse of naked chest open to Barbara's view. Although she had seen Steve in much less, the sight of his naked chest in broad daylight caused her mouth to go dry. My God, I want him, she thought, I want him to make love to me all night long.

They feasted on sandwiches and Barbara's beloved chips, complete with a spicy bean dip that Barbara had found in the cabinet. They drank a little wine and talked of many things, leaving Barbara amazed and delighted that they had much, much more in common than just tennis. Their tastes in movies and music were similar although not identical, and they both adored Ray Bradbury and old reruns of *Star Trek*. Steve promised to take Barbara to the new *Star Trek* movie that was due to come out the next month. He was surprised to find out that Barbara loved the symphony as much as he did, but that she seldom went because her beeper disturbed the patrons around her. As they argued spiritedly over a political difference of opinion, Barbara thought suddenly how well suited they would have been as a married couple. They had enough things in common to get along well, but enough differences to make life interesting. Steve would be fun to live with as well as make love to. Sighing, Barbara pushed those thoughts away. It's too bad, she told herself. With both of them feeling the way they did about marriage, that lovely compatibility would go to waste. What a shame, Barbara thought wistfully. What a crying shame.

They waited until the rain let up, then Barbara drove back to Steve's in the soft mist. "Coming in?" he asked quietly when she didn't kill her engine in front of his house.

"I'll go on home and get on dry clothes," Barbara said. "Are we going out?"

93

Steve nodded. "I want to take you somewhere really nice," he murmured as he kissed her lips softly. "We'll go to the best."

Barbara nodded. "Pick me up in a couple of hours, then," she said as she drove away. How lovely! she thought as she made her way home in the heavy traffic. Steve actually thought of an evening together as a special occasion! In some ways he was taking this affair more seriously than she was.

Back at her own home Barbara took a long, leisurely soak in a hot tub, delicately scented with her favorite sophisticated perfume. Then she curled her hair and spent time meticulously applying her makeup. She looked at herself critically. Steve had never seen this glamorous, sophisticated Barbara with her hair swirling around her face in a fluffy cloud of platinum and her face glowing from the tinted hues expertly used. He had seen her wilted and in jeans and with buttons missing, but he had never seen her decked out for an evening on the town. In fact she had not dressed up like this since she had attended that last charity banquet with Wayne. Barbara's hand froze halfway to her mouth. Now, what on earth had caused her to think of a thing like that? Tonight had nothing to do with her marriage. She was dressing up to please Steve, and she hoped as she pulled on the new blue knit dress that the effort was worth it.

Barbara had not needed to worry. Steve's eyes widened into huge hazel circles when she answered the door. He held her gently at arm's length and stared at her in amazement. "I knew you were beautiful," he breathed into her hair as he drew her to him, "but I didn't really realize until now just how beautiful you are."

Barbara looked with breath-shortening excitement at Steve, dressed in a black dinner jacket. "You aren't so bad yourself," she murmured.

Steve kissed her once, then followed her into the living room, where a bottle of her favorite white wine sat on the table. He filled her glass and thrust it into her hand. "Drink up," he said lightly. "I have reservations for eight."

Barbara finished her drink and together they walked to Steve's car. The moon was peeking through the clouds and the breeze was refreshingly cool after the rain. Steve drove a short distance to a highly acclaimed country club, where a uniformed parking attendant spirited away the Jaguar. Barbara admired the beautiful old club, built in the twenties but cared for lovingly. "I'm glad you like it," Steve said as their waiter seated them. "I'll bring you here often."

Barbara nodded wordlessly and studied her menu. She was glad that she would be coming here often as Steve's guest. She selected a filet of sole and Steve ordered prime rib. They talked and chatted throughout their meal, but, as had been the case last week, their minds were on the evening to come. Barbara's fingers trembled as she thought of Steve possessing her again and again, with just the two of them and no intrusions from the outside world. Was he as excited as she was? She sipped her wine and looked over the rim at Steve, who was whispering to the waiter. In a moment the waiter returned with a magnum of champagne. "This is an occasion to celebrate," Steve said solemnly as he poured champagne for them both. "To us."

"To us," Barbara said as she lifted her glass in toast. He was as excited as she was, and what a lovely way to show it! she thought as she sipped the bubbling beverage. Whatever else could be said about Steve Sullivan, the man had class.

Catching the look of anticipation in Barbara's eyes, Steve paid the waiter and escorted Barbara to the car. On the way to her condominium they said very little, but their clasped hands in the middle of the seat spoke volumes. He parked his car in front of her condo, but did not immediately jump out. Instead he continued to hold Barbara's hand as they stared up at the silver moon peeking out from behind the clouds. Slowly Steve reached out and drew Barbara close to him, running his fingers through the curling disarray of her long hair and kissing each eyelid tenderly, causing warm shivers of pleasure to course through

Barbara, right down to her toes. "If I don't stop, we won't get out of this car before morning," he murmured in her ear.

Barbara opened her door and met Steve in front of the car. He swung her up into his arms and carried her the short distance to the front door, putting her down so that she could fish her key out of her purse. He unlocked and opened the front door, then reached out and swung Barbara back into his arms. "What are you doing?" she demanded as Steve strode through the house.

"Me Tarzan, you Jane," Steve growled as he shouldered open the door to her room. He looked around Barbara's opulent bedroom, only a little messy tonight. "I'll bet Tarzan never had it this fancy in the jungle!"

Barbara kicked off her shoes as Steve strode toward the bed. "Don't!" she squealed as he dumped her in the middle of the bed. "We'll mess up the covers!"

"That's the idea." Steve laughed menacingly as he stripped off his tie and jacket. Barbara could see that his hands were trembling, as were her own. Off came his shirt and then, naked to the waist, Steve sat down on the edge of the bed. He slipped off his shoes and socks, then Barbara reached forward and wrapped her arms around Steve's broad frame, locking her hands together in front of his chest. She nibbled the sensitive skin at his nape until he moaned. "Just let me get out of these damned pants," he protested as he unfastened the belt.

"Who's stopping you?" Barbara asked innocently as she continued her assault on his neck.

Awkwardly Steve wiggled out of his pants and briefs; then in a lightning motion he had Barbara flat on her back, pinned to the mattress. "Who's stopping you?" he mimicked as he covered her throat with feather-light kisses. "Okay, now it's your turn. You undress."

"No way," Barbara said demurely. "That's your job." Her eyes drank in the sensual perfection of his naked form.

"Very well," Steve mocked as he reached for her zipper. "I'm not responsible for the shape you find your clothes in tomorrow

96

morning." In spite of his warning he was surprisingly careful with her clothes, removing first her dress and laying it across a chair. He then kissed every inch of her neck and throat and midriff that her dress had exposed, setting Barbara on fire with his moist, eager lips. Next came her slip and pantyhose, carefully removed from her trembling legs as Steve sensuously massaged her calves and thighs, turning her firm limbs into jelly. Then, as Barbara waited expectantly, Steve unhooked her bra and let her firm breasts spill out, then pitched the bra across the floor. His eyes widening at the sight of her naked breasts, he lowered his head and took a nipple into his mouth, wetting it with a gentle sucking motion until it was hard and sensitive. Barbara moaned and arched her body closer to his, delighting in everything he was doing to her and wanting him to do more. "Wait, my love," Steve whispered gently. "Let's take our time. We have all night."

Willing herself not to hurry their passion, Barbara reached out slowly and trailed her hands down Steve's chest until they encircled his waist. She wanted to touch him, to explore him, to learn every spot and nuance of his body. Steve was right. They did have all night, and it would take her that long to touch and probe and caress him to her complete satisfaction. She gloried in the feel of the lean, sensuous body that was above hers, and she wanted to know it as intimately as she did her own. Lightly, so as not to hurt him, she leaned forward and nipped Steve's shoulder with her teeth, gasping when he pushed her back into the mattress and caressed her other breast, taking the nipple into his mouth and rolling it gently as spasms of delight shot through her body. "Did you like that?" he asked hoarsely.

Barbara nodded wordlessly, reveling in the delight of Steve exploring her body the same way that she wanted to explore his. His mouth and hands trailed lower, finding the elastic of her panties and carefully drawing them down her legs. Thus freed, Barbara's legs moved restlessly under Steve's, trying to complete the union that would be so fulfilling when it came. Gently he pushed her legs open, but instead of possessing her, as Barbara had expected, he let his mouth nibble its way to her navel and taste her, his tongue sliding around the inside. Although delighting in his attentions, Barbara felt she had to protest. "I want to touch you."

"Not yet," Steve murmured against her stomach. "You'll have plenty of opportunity to give me pleasure later." He slid his warm fingers between Barbara's soft, silky thighs, finding her warmth and stroking it gently as Barbara's legs slowly relaxed. "I love to feel you respond to me the way you do," Steve murmured as she whispered incoherently.

Sensing her deep arousal, Steve moved over her, filling her completely and with a thoroughness that made Barbara gasp. She arched upward to meet him, reveling in the feeling of his body united with hers. Slowly at first, then building momentum, they moved together. Barbara felt that she and Steve were on a mysterious voyage to a destination that both had glimpsed but that neither had seen clearly. As their motions became more passionate, Barbara twisted under Steve in a rocking motion in rhythm with him, feeling the pressure building in her midsection, pressure that had to give way or she would scream. When it finally gave way she did scream, so shaken was she by the delicious waves that spread throughout her body. Steve stiffened and his body arched into hers, giving her the ultimate gift that a man could give a woman.

Slowly they drifted back down to earth, their bodies a tangled mass of legs and arms. Steve carefully drew away from Barbara and pulled a strand of her hair out of his mouth. "Happy?" he asked softly.

"You know I am," Barbara said as she wiped the sweat from Steve's brow. And she was. They had not repeated their mistake of last week, but had savored each other completely.

"And that's only the start," Steve whispered as he reached over and kissed Barbara on the temple. "We have all night, remember?"

"We can't possibly do any more!" Barbara protested.

"Want to bet?" Steve laughed as he turned Barbara over and kissed her lovingly.

Barbara lost count of the times and the ways that they gave pleasure to each other throughout that night of discovery. They shared a passion and a tenderness that she had never known before, and Barbara suspected from Steve's response that this depth of passion was new to him, too. They gave and they received and they shared as man and woman were meant to, and in so doing became bound to each other in a mysterious new covenant. Finally, as dawn streaked the sky and lightened the windows, and they lay exhausted in one another's arms, Barbara suggested that they sleep for a few hours. Steve, tired and content, agreed. "But before you go to sleep, Barbara, I have something I want to ask you."

"Sure, Steve, what is it?" Barbara asked, already half asleep.

Steve hesitated for a moment, as though he was unsure what to say. "Would you be willing to go away with me on your next weekend off?" he finally blurted.

Barbara raised her head and looked at him. It seemed like such a simple request, why had Steve hesitated to ask her? "Of course, I'd love to," she replied sleepily. "Where do you want to go?"

"Maybe to the coast," Steve suggested diffidently. Now that he had asked her, his unease was gone and he seemed totally unconcerned about her reply. It was almost as though he had not asked her the question that he had originally intended to ask.

"Sounds lovely," Barbara murmured as she snuggled back down into the bed and curled her arm across Steve's chest. She wondered for a moment why it was so important to Steve that she go with him, but sleep claimed her exhausted body and she thought no more.

CHAPTER SIX

"You can stop jumping around over there," Steve said dryly as Barbara wiggled in the bucket seat and peered out of the windows expectantly. "We're almost there."

"Oh, hush, I'll wiggle if I want to," Barbara replied as her eyes darted from one view to another. It had been several years since she had been to Corpus Christi, and she wanted to see the pretty little city again. In fact, she had begged Steve to take the bridge into Corpus and take Ocean Drive through town so that she could see the harbor and the bay. Even though it would take them longer this way, Steve had patiently agreed to the detour.

Barbara had gazed eagerly at the sailboats in the harbor, masts swaying in the soft autumn breeze, the early October wind still hot on the Gulf. Corpus Christi Bay was beautiful, as was the rest of the Texas coastline, and Barbara breathed in the tangy salt air. Yes, she was wiggling a little, but she was not impatient, just excited about the coming weekend with Steve.

They had not seen much of each other in the last two weeks, not since her last weekend off. Steve had spent part of the first week out of town on business, and Barbara had been at the hospital late on the nights that he was in town. Last weekend had been shot by the beeper, as usual, and Steve had spent Sunday with Scooter, anyway. They had managed to get together for one night earlier this week, but they both were so tired that they made love once and fell into an exhausted sleep, only to be aroused by the telephone at four in the morning by another expectant mother in labor. But Barbara had rested last night, and she and Steve had two whole days to relax and explore and make love together. She needed it. They both did.

100

Steve drove back out to the highway that led to Padre Island and consulted a travel brochure. "Look for the Drifting Sands condominium complex," he said as they drove over the causeway that would take them to Padre Island.

Barbara watched the signs carefully, and was rewarded about a mile down the island by a large sign with DRIFTING SANDS boldly painted in red. Steve turned into the gravel driveway leading into the condominiums and parked in front of the office. He disappeared into the office and came back momentarily with a set of keys. "We're on the second floor," he said as he drove to their parking space. "I hope that's all right."

"Lovely," Barbara assured him. "The view will be better." She followed Steve up a set of outdoor steps and into their condominium. It was not overly large, but no effort had been spared to make it luxurious. Rich bright fabrics covered the furniture and the floors of the living room and a huge king-size bed graced the bedroom. The tiny kitchen was completely equipped with everything a cook could possibly want or need. Obligingly Barbara unloaded the groceries into the refrigerator while Steve brought in their suitcases. He placed them on the racks and opened his, fishing out a bright orange swimsuit. Unselfconsciously he stripped and pulled it on as Barbara's eyes widened in appreciation. She had not yet become used to the sight of his naked body. And I hope I never get completely used to it, she thought as she found her own suit.

Oh, no, Barbara wailed inwardly as she pulled on her white bikini. She had bought it several years ago when she had been a few pounds lighter, and now it was not only out of style, but it was too small. Her breasts spilled out of the top, and the tiny brief was tightly plastered to her bottom. She peered out of the window and bit back a howl of dismay. Every other woman on the beach in front of the condo was wearing a fashionable maillot. Damn! Why couldn't she have taken time to get a new suit?

"I'm not sure I want to let you go out there like that," Steve said slowly as he surveyed Barbara's barely clad form.

101

"I don't blame you," she said quietly, cut to the quick. Wayne had been ashamed of her clothes, too. "I look pretty bad." She looked at him sadly.

"No, that ain't the problem, lady," Steve replied as he came to her, running his hands down her bare arms. "It's not that you look so bad. It's that you look so damn good!" He kissed her roughly, then set her away from him. "Let's get on out there and swim this morning, because the sun will burn you too badly after lunch." Steve loped out the bedroom door, leaving Barbara staring after him in astonishment. He honestly thought her old bathing suit looked good!

They swam and frolicked in the water for two hours, the gentle morning sun caressing Barbara's skin and not burning it. The beach was only moderately crowded at this time of year, and she and Steve were able to swim with relative freedom out to the barrier floats and back. He volunteered to teach her to body-surf and showed her how to lie low on the waves and allow the surf to propel her to shore. She quickly mastered the skill and he proclaimed her one of the quickest studies he had ever seen. Barbara in turn introduced Steve to the pleasures of building a truly monumental sand castle, with turrets and a drawbridge and a moat that they filled with water, only to watch the water seep back into the sand. As the sun drew higher in the sky, Barbara pulled on an old T-shirt for protection against burn and they combed the beach for shells, finding two really beautiful specimens, and picked up an irate hermit crab by mistake. Finally Steve reached out and touched Barbara's nose gently. "If we don't get you off this beach, you're going to fry."

"I guess you're right," Barbara admitted, knowing that her sunscreen was probably almost gone. They walked hand in hand to the condominium. Caught up in watching the other swimmers on the beach, Barbara did not realize until they were almost back at the condominium that Steve had become strangely quiet. She looked over at him and was surprised by the faraway, reflective look on his face. "Steve, are you all right?" she asked.

"What? Oh, sure, I'm fine," Steve assured her as his mind returned to the present. "You know, Dr. Weimer, you need a bath." He looked down at her salt- and sand-encrusted body.

"So do you, Mr. Sullivan," she replied. "Care to conserve water with me?"

"I thought you'd never ask!" Steve replied as he took her hand and they ran up the stairs. They stripped off their sandy suits and dumped them in the sink, and Steve turned on the shower. "Come on in, it's perfect!" he shouted over the sound of the running water.

"Sure I—YOW!" Barbara cried. "That water's cold! Turn on the hot!"

"No way." Steve laughed as he hauled Barbara back under the cool spray. The water was not all that cold, but nevertheless large goose-pimples popped up all over her body. "This is good for you," he continued as he squirted shampoo into her hair and washed out all the salt and sand.

"Good for me, my foot," Barbara complained, soaping Steve's muscled chest. "I'm not an Eskimo."

"It will get up your circulation," Steve reminded her. He quickly soaped her body, lingering on her breasts and hips just long enough to remind her of her femininity. He held her under the spray until the soap was rinsed off, then pushed her out of the shower and stood in the full spray while Barbara toweled herself dry. "Ah, this is heaven," he murmured, the cool water running down his naked body.

"Takes all kinds, I guess," Barbara muttered as she dried her body and rung out her hair. "Hey, what are we doing this afternoon?"

"How would you like to go to Padre? We can rent a Jeep and go down the beach past the end of the road." Steve stuck his head out of the shower and grabbed a towel. "Or would you rather go back into Corpus?"

"Padre," Barbara replied instantly. "We can go back into

Corpus tonight." She peered into the mirror. "My face got red," she mused as she fingered her pink nose.

Steve's face appeared behind hers in the mirror. "That's all right. You're just as beautiful with a red nose as with a white one." He kissed the side of her neck tenderly and swatted her bare bottom gently. "Go get ready before I decide to make love to you all afternoon."

In a very few minutes, clad in jeans and T-shirts, Steve and Barbara set out in a rented Jeep to explore Padre Island. Barbara watched with eager eyes as they drove down the long, narrow island that separated the Texas coast from the Gulf of Mexico. Condominiums lined the beach for the first three or four miles of the island, then abruptly all development stopped and the beach was left in its natural state. Steve stopped at the ranger's station and picked up a few brochures that Barbara leafed through as they drove down the beach. A few miles into the National Seashore, Steve pulled over. "I want to look at these dunes," he volunteered as he hopped out of the Jeep.

Together they explored the dunes, trudging through the thick loose sand thrown up by the wind coming off the Gulf. Much to her delight Barbara spotted several tiny sea birds that lived in the dunes. They returned to the Jeep and drove on down the highway, past Malachite Beach and the public one, and on to the end of the highway. Steve drove to the end of the road and onto the flat, damp sand. "What are you doing?" Barbara demanded. "Won't this hurt the beach?"

Steve shook his head. "A limited number of four-wheel-drive vehicles are authorized to come in here. We're fine." He drove on for two or three miles, carefully dodging driftwood and the occasional campsite until they had reached a deserted stretch of sand.

Eagerly Barbara jumped out and ran toward the water. "This is marvelous!" she exclaimed. "We should have waited to swim here."

"This sun would have cooked you," Steve protested as he

pulled a picnic basket from the back of the Jeep. "Surprise! I brought lunch."

"I'd forgotten about lunch," Barbara said honestly. She squinted up at the sky. "I guess you're right about the sun."

Steve spread out a large blanket for the two of them, and soon they were greedily eating ham sandwiches and potato chips that Steve had brought from Houston. Barbara munched her chips and stared out at the water, mesmerized by the rhythmic pounding of the waves. I'm at peace, she thought, for the first time in a long time. The pain of her divorce was finally gone, she was away from her professional responsibilities for once, and she was with a wonderful man. Oh, sweet bliss! She turned to Steve and was surprised to spot a look of concentration, almost a frown, on his face. "Steve?" she asked softly.

Immediately Steve came out of his reverie, and the frowning look was replaced by a lazy smile. "Care for some dessert?" he asked wickedly.

"In broad daylight?" Barbara teased. "I don't think so. This is a little public."

"I guess you're right," Steve replied. "But you do realize that I intend to repay you later for saying no to me now." He leered suggestively at Barbara and she had a very good idea what her payment would be. They cleaned up the remnants from their lunch and spent the better part of the afternoon exploring. A national seashore, the island was completely protected from development except for small stretches at either end, and the long island beach was completely unspoiled by man. Barbara found more shells to add to her collection, and Steve poked around examining the driftwood and the marsh grasses on the dunes. Once Barbara found him looking at her speculatively, as though he were wondering something about her, but when he caught her eye the look was quickly replaced by a lazy smile. Barbara in turn was finding herself drawn more and more to Steve, feeling an emotional closeness to him as well as a physical bond. You got lucky when this one came along, she told herself. You got real lucky.

Finally they decided that they had explored enough and started back to the condominium. As they were leaving the park, Barbara spotted a souvenir shop just outside the rangers' station. "Oh, Steve, let's stop here!" she exclaimed. "I love beachcomber shops."

"It's just a tourist trap," Steve complained, but nevertheless he obligingly pulled over and stopped in front of the shop. Barbara hopped out and went inside. The owner, a leftover hippie with a vague expression on his face, motioned to Barbara to look around. Eagerly she poked through the piles of shells and starfish and tacky painted ashtrays. Steve joined her and together they examined the merchandise. They howled with glee at the T-shirt that had ten toes up and ten toes down that said THE DAMN SAND GETS INTO EVERYTHING AT PORT ARANSAS! and sincerely admired some large conch shells that had been imported from the South Seas but were still beautiful. Impulsively Barbara picked up the prettiest shell and bought it, presenting it to Steve as a remembrance of the weekend. In turn Steve bought Barbara a carved black-coral ring, inexpensive but pretty. Before she could stop him, Steve picked up her left hand and slipped the ring onto her third finger. Barbara tensed and her eyes grew wide. Then Steve, realizing that the ring was too big for her third finger, transferred it to her second finger. Barbara expelled the breath that she had been unconsciously holding and sincerely admired the striking ring. She had not liked the ring at all when it was on her third finger, but on her second finger it was beautiful!

It was after five when they finally returned to the condominium. After her experience with Steve that morning Barbara quickly offered to let him shower first. "Do you want me to start cooking supper?" she asked as Steve disappeared into the bathroom.

"No, I thought we'd drive back into Corpus and eat at one of

106

those fancy restaurants on the bay," Steve said. He stuck his head out of the shower. "Are you sure that you don't want to shower with me?"

"No," Barbara replied quickly. They would just have to waste the water!

She wandered around the condo, finally ending up on the small balcony overlooking the beach. A few stragglers were still sunning or swimming, but most of the people had gone in, and Barbara could smell steaks grilling not far away. This is wonderful, she thought again. Peace and relaxation. She dropped into a folding chair and propped her feet on the rail. I don't have a care in the world. She ran her fingers through her hair and stared out at the pounding waves. But is Steve as happy as I am? she wondered. If she didn't know better, she would think that he was really concerned about something.

Steve stuck his head around the sliding door. "The Eskimos are through," he volunteered.

Barbara jumped, startled. "You're always scaring me to death!" she complained crossly. She stripped off her clothes on the way to the bathroom, leaving a trail of garments littering her path, and shut the door behind her. She ran the shower as hot as she could stand and drenched herself, then stepped out and opened the bathroom door to let out the steam.

"What did you do, take a steam bath?" Steve complained as white fog poured out of the open door. Barbara hummed happily as she toweled dry her hair. "Where do you want these?" Steve asked pointedly, holding up the clothes she had dropped on the floor.

"Anywhere you want to put them," Barbara said absently as Steve stared at the clothes in his hand. "Over there in the corner will be all right."

"I'm glad I'm not your maid," Steve grumbled as he folded her dirty clothes neatly and put them with his own.

The restaurant Steve selected was on the top floor of Corpus

Christi's finest hotel. Barbara gazed out the window at the bay, bathed in the deepening purple dusk. The wind was picking up although the night was still warm, and the whitecaps appeared blue in the fading light. A combo was warming up for the evening, and the other elegant diners were making their selections as Barbara and Steve were. Barbara had brought with her a white silk shirt and burgundy pants in velvet, neither new but still passable, and she wore only the coral ring for adornment. More casually dressed than he would have been in Houston, Steve was still easily the most striking man in the room in a cream silk shirt and matching slacks. They placed their order, a Chateaubriand that they would share, and Steve took her hand in his, twisting the coral ring idly. "Glad you came?" he asked quietly.

"You know I am," Barbara replied warmly. She met Steve's gentle gaze and smiled at him dazzlingly.

The band struck up a recent western hit, and Steve took Barbara's hand and led her to the dance floor. Although she was rusty, Barbara felt herself following Steve's expert lead through the lively number and was sorry when it was over. Steve led her back to the table just as their very young waiter arrived with the thick steak. Barbara watched, fascinated and a little nervous, as the waiter poured wine over the meat and lit it, then, after the wine had burned off, cut the steak into thin strips. Carefully he served each plate a portion of meat and then loaded the plates with succulent vegetables. As the young man left, Steve expelled a breath. "He was awfully young to be playing with matches," he said sarcastically, trying to hide his uneasiness.

"Oh, hush, he did fine," Barbara replied as she bit into her steak.

They ate in comfortable silence, the silence of two people who were in unspoken rapport with one another and who were comfortable in that state. The daylight was completely gone by now, and the lights twinkled from the boats and the buoys in the bay. The water, less rough than it would have been on the open coastline, still slapped the pier soundly. The band was playing a mellow love song, and Barbara sighed. The evening was perfect! She turned to Steve, wanting to share her feelings with him, and saw him staring out at the water with an absent expression on his face. He's doing it again, Barbara thought as she ate another bite of meat. He's thinking about something, and it's worrying him. Was it his business? His son? Something she didn't know about? Something she could help him with?

Steve looked over and saw Barbara staring at him, and immediately his face lit up in a gentle smile. "Care to dance again?" he asked softly.

Barbara nodded and slid out of her seat. They clung together tightly during the slow, sexy number, Barbara shamelessly devouring Steve with her eyes. She remembered the night of passion they had shared in her bed and she shivered with the thought of sharing that bliss again tonight.

The music stopped. Unwillingly they drew apart, each loath to leave the other's embrace. They danced several more numbers, all slow romantic waltzes, holding each other as close as decency permitted, swaying together in sensuous abandon. Finally, when the band took a break, Steve signaled the waiter and asked for the check. "Do you mind?" he asked as Barbara's eyebrows rose. Why did he want the evening to end? The night was still young. "I have something else planned before we turn in."

"Of course not," Barbara replied, willing to leave with him but mystified. Steve led her out of the hotel and to his car, and they drove back the way they had come. As Steve pulled into the condo parking lot, Barbara eyed him suspiciously. Just what did he have in mind?

Barbara climbed out of the car and Steve took her hand and led her toward the Jeep. "I really do have something else in mind," he promised Barbara with a grin as she became more and more baffled. They hopped into the Jeep and roared away, taking the highway toward the National Seashore. Soon they were beyond the lights of civilization, the only light coming from the occasional campsite and the full moon that had risen over the horizon.

When they came to the end of the highway, Steve confidently pulled onto the beach and continued down the wet sand. Slowly and carefully he drove past a couple of campsites and on down the deserted beach. When they were probably a mile past the last campsite, Steve stopped the Jeep and killed the engine. The only sounds they could hear were the roar of the wind in their ears and the rough surf pounding the shore. "We couldn't swim out here this afternoon," Steve said softly. "How about now?"

Barbara smiled a slow, womanly smile. She stared at the rolling waves. She had never swum nude before, nor had she gone swimming in the ocean at night, but why not? How intimate that would be, to share the ocean naked with Steve! "Without our suits?" she asked softly.

In answer to her question Steve unbuttoned her shirt. After she shrugged her shoulders out of it, she in turn unbuttoned Steve's shirt and slid it off his shoulders. He pulled Barbara to him, reaching behind her and unhooking her bra, letting it fall on the seat. Touching one moon-dappled nipple with his palm, he closed his fingers over it as it hardened in his hand. Unconsciously Barbara thrust her chest forward, eager to meet his sensual touch. Slowly he slid his hand across to her other breast, palming the nipple until it, too, was hard. Then Steve withdrew his hands from Barbara's body and opened the door of the Jeep. "We have all night again, remember?" he reminded her as Barbara's expressive face protested his withdrawal.

Barbara slid out of the seat and stood in the soft sand. Steve had already shed the rest of his clothes and was running for the water, his magnificent body illuminated by the glow of the full moon. Barbara slipped out of her shoes and her pants, last of all sliding down her panties, and then she was running toward the water as well, loving the feel of the wind on the most intimate parts of her body. The sensation of complete freedom was almost overwhelming. Steve was already waist deep in the pounding waves, his broad back soundly buffeted by the tide. Barbara splashed into the churning surf, her naked body delighting in the surprising warmth of the water. She walked out to where Steve was standing, watching her glide toward him in the moonlight.

"You look like a Greek goddess," he murmured as he caught her close. "Or maybe a mermaid from Atlantis." Steve ran his hands over Barbara's hair, wet at the tips, and lowered his hands onto her hips. Tiny shivers of pleasure coursed through Barbara as the waves pounded her back and Steve's touch worked magic on her body. She reached forward and shamelessly drew him closer to her, their hips thrust together in provocative intimacy. She swayed closer to him and he met her mouth with his own. Hotly their tongues tangled and fenced, as first Steve was the aggressor, then Barbara. He pulled his mouth from her, then lowered his lips to her neck, nibbling a sensual trail to her earlobe. Barbara lightly nipped Steve's chin and was rewarded by a gentle bite on her ear, the slight pain a sensual pleasure. Determinedly Steve thrust Barbara away, leaving her feeling momentarily bereft. "Let's swim," he commanded gruffly.

Why does he want to swim? Barbara wondered as Steve dived into the water. Why don't we just make love, like we both want to? But as she watched Steve disappear into the inky depths, she became conscious of the sensual touch of the water on her body, the soft kiss of the moon's light on her arms and breasts, the seductive whisper of the wind in her ear. "We're making love with the night and the ocean," Barbara whispered to herself as another soft wave caressed her back. "Then we will make love to each other with all the fullness nature bestows."

Steve surfaced several feet away. "Come on, swim with me!" he called to her. Delighting in the myriad sensations that were assaulting her senses, Barbara took out after him, squealing with feigned surprise when Steve grabbed her around her waist and ducked her thoroughly. She retaliated by splashing water in his face and breaking away from him as he tried to wipe the water

111

from his eyes. "I'll get you for that!" he exclaimed, trying to see her through the film of water.

Quickly Barbara ducked back under the surface and swam away from him, coming up several feet away, taunting him. He lunged toward her and she swam away again. She played cat and mouse with him, delighting in the coy game of pursuit, until she gave him just a little too much time to find her, and suddenly he had his arms around her before she could get away. He picked her up by the waist and lifted her high out of the water, then threw her far out and laughed when she landed on her bottom. She sank under the waves, deliberately not coming up when she knew Steve expected her to. In a few seconds he was beside her, hauling her up out of the water quickly and shaking her a little when she laughed out loud. "Serves you right," she sputtered as she leaned forward and wrapped her arms around his shoulders.

Steve grasped Barbara around the waist and pulled her closer to him. "You scared me to death!" he protested as his lips met her own. Their play in the water together had built up their excitement to an almost intolerable level, and their passion could no longer be denied. Their mouths and bodies met and mingled, and Steve's strength made Barbara aware of his unleashed desire. The warm water lapped their bodies gently until a particularly large wave almost knocked them over. "We'd better get to a safer spot," he murmured as he pulled his lips from Barbara's.

He picked her up and carried her only as far as the shore, where they sank down onto the wet sand. They would complete their union here on the beach, under the light of the moon, the primitive setting releasing their wildest desires. They were half in and half out of the water, with the tail ends of the waves wetting their feet and legs. Pushing Barbara back on the sand, Steve stroked and caressed her body with familiar intimacy, remembering all the secret touches that drove her to distraction. Barbara arched upward to touch him, feel him, know him as she had never known a man before. They rolled together in the sand, unmindful of the gritty coating on their legs and bodies, only conscious of the wild desire that was driving them onward. Finally, as the flames soared out of control, Steve moved over Barbara and possessed her body with his own.

Perhaps it was the moonlight, or maybe it was the natural setting—they would never know—but they made love with savage abandon. Totally uninhibited, totally in accord, they moved as one, Steve setting the rhythm until Barbara rolled him onto his back and caressed his shoulders, moving her tongue over his chest and hardened nipples. She slowly circled his warm skin with her fingers, finding the hollows of his hips, and lowered her head. She gently nestled against his body and as she lovingly brushed her mouth across his sensitive flesh she felt Steve tremble and moan, grabbing her hair in his powerful hands. She kissed his fingertips and slid up his body to meet his mouth and, pressing into him, bore him down into the sand.

She exulted in the feeling of giving, of taking, of loving this man who was glorying in their passion. As overpowering as an ancient goddess, Barbara made love to Steve with unrestrained delight, the silent moon in the sky her only witness. As sensation mounted, she could feel Steve tense and arch into her, and when his fulfillment came Barbara dug her palms into his shoulders and threw back her head and whimpered, her own release triggered by his.

Exhausted, she let herself collapse into Steve's waiting arms. She was shaking and trembling from the force of her need, stunned by the depth of her own emotion. "I didn't know I was capable of that," she whispered in an unsteady voice.

Steve rolled her onto her side and kissed her trembling lips gently. "I didn't know it could be like that, either," he whispered brokenly. "My God, Barbara, I love you!"

"Oh, Steve, I love you, too!" she whispered in wonder. And she did. She didn't know when or how it had happened, but she did love Steve. She had fallen in love again! And I'm glad, I'm so glad, she thought as she remembered with amusement her promises to herself not to get romantically involved with Steve.

How ridiculous she had been! Of course they loved each other! They were lovers, weren't they? Barbara stared up at the moon as two small tears of joy collected in her eyes and ran down her cheeks. She had never thought that she could be this happy! Sighing, she reached out and kissed Steve's lips tenderly. "Oh, yes," she whispered, "I do love you."

"We'd better rinse the sand off," Steve said later. They had sat together on the sand for a long time, staring into the waves and talking quietly, both delighted with the love they had discovered in one another. Barbara nodded and together they walked back into the churning surf, quickly washing the dirt from their hair and their bodies. Steve had remembered to bring a couple of towels, so they were able to pat themselves dry and put their clothes back on, although neither bothered with shoes. They drove back to the condominium and Steve showered off the salt while Barbara prepared a midnight snack of cheese sandwiches. Steve waited graciously while Barbara rinsed off in the shower, then, laughing and giggling like a couple of teen-agers, they sat on the living-room floor in front of the window and ate their snack, watching the waves pound the beach. Steve found Barbara's hairbrush and helped her brush out the damp tangles, and she in turn gave him an expert massage with her knowing, loving fingers. "You mustn't stop," Steve murmured as Barbara drew away from him.

"It's late," she replied, standing up and reaching out her hand to Steve. He pulled himself up and then swung Barbara back into his arms and carried her to the bedroom, where he gently laid her on the bed and untied the straps of her nightgown, allowing the soft fabric to fall down around her waist. Pulling off his own robe, Steve sank down beside Barbara and buried his lips between her breasts. "I just can't get enough of you," he murmured as he captured her lips with his own and bore her down into the covers. He covered her face and her body with soft, gentle kisses and caresses, and Barbara felt desire rise in her again, desire less

114

savage than the longing she had felt on the beach, but a drive deep and strong nevertheless.

Barbara had thought that all her passion had been spent, but she was wrong. Slowly, tenderly, Steve aroused her again. They were not rough and demanding with each other as they had been earlier in the moonlight, but slowly, coaxingly, leading one another on as the fire between them built and spread to their fingers and toes, they became one again, and once more rose to the heights together. As they gradually returned to reality, Steve pulled Barbara onto his chest and buried her chin in her hair. "I love you, my pagan goddess," he whispered.

"I love you, too," she replied.

"I guess we'd better get packing," Barbara said reluctantly as she pulled on her jeans for the drive back to Houston. It was late, and Steve had wanted to be on the road before dusk. It didn't look as if they were going to make it, however. They had played in the water all morning and had driven into the old section of Corpus Christi that afternoon, visiting a few more of Barbara's beloved souvenir shops, although neither of them bought any more remembrances. Barbara looked down at the ring on her middle finger. It looked good there, and she would always treasure it, not for its monetary value, but as a token of the weekend that she and Steve had discovered their love for each other. Now they would have to hurry if they were going to be back in Houston before eleven or twelve.

Steve produced two canvas bags and presented one to Barbara. "Bring the dirty pile here," he commanded. Together they sorted their dirty clothes and stuffed them into the bags. That done, Barbara sighed and sneaked out on the balcony while Steve put the bags in the car. He joined her on the balcony, and in spite of the packing that had not been done, he stood with her, gazing out at the water.

"I wish it didn't have to end," Barbara said, sighing, thinking of the busy practice that she had to go back to.

"It doesn't," Steve said slowly. "Not if we don't want it to."

"Oh, sure," Barbara said lightly. "We can stay down here forever."

"We can't stay here forever, but it still doesn't have to end," Steve replied gently. Barbara turned and looked at him, wondering at the seriousness in his voice. His face had that intent expression that she had seen several times already this weekend, but this time Steve made no effort to hide it. "I mean it, Barbara, it doesn't have to end. Marry me."

"What?" Barbara asked, stunned, not sure that she had heard him right.

"You heard me, Barbara. I want to marry you."

CHAPTER SEVEN

Barbara stared at Steve with wariness on her face. The man was kidding. He had to be kidding. He was as unwilling to marry as she was. Slowly she turned her head and faced him, a slight smile on her face. "No, I don't think so," she said lightly. "I don't have time this week."

She turned to go into the living room, but Steve reached out and grabbed her around the wrist, holding her firmly as he swung her around. He looked into her eyes with a tender expression on his face. "I'm not kidding," he said softly. "I've thought about it all weekend. I love you and want to marry you."

He really meant it! My God, he really wanted to marry her! Stunned, Barbara stared at him stupidly. "You mean you want to marry me?" she croaked, unsteadily. Steve nodded. "Oh my God, no!" she cried as she broke away from Steve's firm grip. She walked into the living room and sat down on the sofa, trembling with shock, her head in her hands. How could she have misjudged him so? She honestly thought that all he wanted was an affair.

Steve followed her and sat down on the floor in front of her. "What's the matter? You're shaking like a leaf!" He knelt by her and shook her slightly. "For God's sake, Barbara, what is it?"

Barbara jumped up from the couch and hurried into the kitchen, trying to calm herself. What in the hell was she going to do now? Her mind on escape, she jerked open the refrigerator and withdrew the fresh vegetables that were left over and stuffed them into the ice chest. She grabbed the carton of milk and turned, bumping smack into Steve, spilling milk all over him. Swearing, he picked up a dishtowel and wiped himself, then took

117

Barbara by the shoulders and turned her to face him. "What in the hell is wrong with you?" he demanded, furious.

"Nothing," Barbara replied too quickly as she packed a can of unopened biscuits into the ice chest. "You wanted to be on the road by nightfall, and it's almost dusk. We need to leave."

"Don't be ridiculous," Steve replied. "Something's got you upset. What is it?"

"I told you, it was nothing!" Barbara snapped back. "I just want to go home, that's all."

Steve leaned against the wall of the kitchen and watched Barbara throw food into the ice chest. "You're not getting out of this kitchen until you tell me what the hell has you so upset," he said grimly.

"It was the joke," Barbara said shortly, hoping against hope she could bluff her way through this. "You said that you wanted to marry me. I don't think that's one bit funny, that's all."

"I wasn't kidding, Barbara," Steve replied with steel in his voice. "I do want to marry you. I want it so bad that my bones ache for you. In fact, I'll go further than that. I have every intention of marrying you, so you'd better get used to the idea."

"Is that a threat?" Barbara asked quietly. Her heart was pounding, and her adrenaline was spurting through every vein.

"A threat?" Steve asked, incredulous. "No, it is not a threat! It is an honest proposal of marriage! A proposal that I want you to say yes to!"

"There's no way I can say yes, Steve," Barbara replied in a thin voice. Oh, God, she thought, how am I ever going to get out of this one? She snapped the lid of the ice chest shut and thrust it into Steve's arms, then fled to the bedroom and slammed the door behind her. Holding her breath until she'd heard the front door open and close, she let out a sigh of relief and gathered up her belongings, stuffing them into her suitcase with lightning speed. When her things were packed, she started loading Steve's, wondering how on earth she was going to ever make him understand. She couldn't marry him! She just couldn't!

She threw the suitcases into the living room and ran into the bathroom, loading her makeup case and Steve's shaving kit as quickly as her trembling fingers would allow, knocking over her shampoo and losing almost half a bottle. She piled the cosmetics case and the shaving kit with the suitcases, then made a quick survey of the condominium. Yes, she had packed everything. The trembling feeling was beginning to subside. Now, if she could just get back to Houston and have a few days to think! She owed Steve an explanation, she knew that. But how do you tell a man you love that you won't marry him? That you're afraid to marry him?

Grabbing up her cases, Barbara opened the front door and collided with Steve. He took the cases out of her hands and led her to the couch. Sitting her down firmly, he seated himself in the opposite chair and eyed her grimly. "You're acting like a fool," he said sharply. "I want to know what the hell is eating you."

"I can't talk about it," Barbara replied. "At least not tonight. I think we'd better go back to Houston." Swallowing a lump in her throat, she continued, "Thank you for the lovely weekend."

"Lovely weekend, hell!" Steve ground out as he lunged toward Barbara. "Look, I'm not sure just what is hacking away at you, but we're not going an inch until you tell me." He gripped her shoulders bruisingly.

"You want to marry me," Barbara whispered.

"Yes, I sure as hell do want to marry you," Steve replied. "So what is the the problem?"

"That is the problem!" Barbara shot back. "You want to marry me!"

Steve looked at her incredulously. "You're acting like this because I want to marry you?" Barbara nodded and Steve ran his hand across his forehead. "It looks like we have a lot to say to each other," he said grimly, "and if we start this conversation here, we won't be back to Houston before morning. Look, you say that you want to get back to Houston. If I take you back, will you *please* explain to me on the way back what your problem is?"

Barbara nodded, chagrined. God knows, she thought, he deserves an explanation. But how can I make him understand? she agonized as Steve locked the condominium and returned the key. Will he understand why I can't marry him? Will he take no for an answer? Barbara suddenly remembered their conversation that day in San Jacinto Park, and fear rose in her. She and Steve had just come to a clashing of wills. Would he indeed prove to be the stronger of the two?

Barbara glanced up to see towering thunderclouds rolling in from the ocean. Hooray, she thought. How appropriate. Steve slammed the door of the office behind him and got into the car, banging the car door angrily. Barbara climbed in beside him and they drove in silence as fat raindrops hit the hood of the car and sizzled on the hot metal.

"So now that we're on our way, why don't you explain to me exactly what's bothering you," Steve said slowly as they drove over the causeway.

"I—I don't know where to start," Barbara stammered.

"How about at the beginning?" Steve asked softly.

Barbara ran her fingers through her hair. "When you first asked me out, I didn't want to go," she said honestly. "I was very attracted to you and that frightened me."

"I remember," Steve said dryly.

"But then the night you took me out—the night Mrs. Valdez died—you said that you had no intention of ever marrying again."

"I never said that," Steve replied slowly.

"Oh, yes, you did," Barbara said sharply. "We were talking about your marriage and you said that you never intended to enter that sort of relationship again. I thought you meant that you never intended to marry again. I thought you would be safe."

"Safe for what?" Steve asked incredulously.

"To have an affair with. To care about. To love," Barbara answered slowly. Oh, no, she was muffing this! That sounded terrible, even to her.

"So I'm not the problem," Steve said. "I thought maybe it was me."

"No, no, it isn't you at all!" Barbara said quickly. "I love you."

"Then why don't you want to marry me?" Steve asked grimly. The rain beat down on the hood of the car, and lightning streaked across the sky, making Barbara jump.

"I can't marry you," Barbara replied. "I can't marry anyone. Steve, all I thought you wanted was an affair. That's all I want. An affair. No more."

"Isn't that a bit different from the line most ladies use?" Steve asked harshly. "I was safe, and you wanted a nice little clandestine affair. Some good sex and some fun. Thanks a lot!" Raw pain threaded through his voice.

"I hardly think that this weekend was sordid," Barbara replied quietly, cut to the heart. Surely he didn't think sex was all she wanted! "Oh, God, Steve, I want love and affection and passion and respect. I want the same things you do. I just don't want marriage."

"Why not?" Steve demanded imperiously. "Most women would be flattered by a sincere proposal of marriage from a man whom they loved and who loved them back. Or didn't the times we shared mean anything to you? Didn't you say you love me? Was I imagining it all?"

"No, you weren't imagining anything," Barbara replied, knotting her fingers together. "Look, Steve, I love you and I want to be a part of your life, but I just can't marry you. I can't marry anyone." She bit her lip.

"Why?" Steve demanded.

She sighed, capitulating. "Look, you deserve the truth."

"I think I do," Steve said mildly.

"You realize that I was married for over six years," Barbara said. Steve nodded. "I understand now that I should never have

121

married Wayne in the first place. I didn't have time to be a decent wife to him. Medicine consumed the lion's share of my existence and left me no time for anything else. I couldn't do all the things that a man expects of a wife." Barbara swallowed a painful lump in her throat. "He found someone else who could do a better job."

"What sort of things weren't you able to do for him?" Steve asked slowly.

"Wayne is an attorney. He needed me to help him entertain clients and assist him socially, and I let him down miserably. I either showed up late and looking dowdy, or I was too busy to even go. The house was never fit to entertain in—it was always a mess, and I just didn't have time to give parties or anything, or even to spend any time with Wayne for fun. And then I didn't have time to have any children. Look, it wasn't Wayne's fault. He had a right to expect those things from his wife. But I couldn't do all those things and still function as a responsible M.D."

"Your marriage broke up over that? Your professional responsibilities versus your role as his wife?" Steve asked.

"Yes," Barbara replied simply. She eyed Steve warily. Would he understand now why she could not marry him?

"So you've decided that marriage is out," Steve concluded.

"Absolutely," Barbara replied emphatically. "The divorce damn near did me in, and I refuse to put myself through another one."

"Then, I don't see what the problem is," Steve said simply. "If you married me there would be no divorce."

"Wayne didn't think there would be one, either," Barbara replied dryly. "You try several years of interrupted evenings, every other weekend shot, midnight calls, ruined parties, and see how long you put up with it."

"I think I've had a pretty good taste of what it would be like married to you," Steve said firmly. "Look, it doesn't bother me, honest to God. Barbara, it wouldn't be like that with me."

"It would be like that with anyone," Barbara said bitterly, twisting a strand of hair around in her fingers.

"Damn it, it would not!" Steve thundered. "I'm not like that at all!"

"Oh, Steve, don't you see? It's all new to you now. Wayne said he would understand, too."

"Are you going to make me pay for another man's mistakes?" Steve said furiously, clenching the steering wheel in his fists. "That's not exactly fair."

"If you want to talk about fair, I'm not the one who changed the rules," she responded with spirit, hitting the seat with her palm.

Steve did not pretend to misunderstand. "Yes, damn it, I changed the rules! I thought you loved me!"

"You idiot, of course I love you!" Barbara cried. "Do you think I would put a man whom I loved through being married to me? It's because I love you that I'm saying no."

"That is ridiculous," Steve replied. "Think about this weekend and what we shared, and then tell me you won't marry me. I'll bet you can't do it."

Barbara leaned her head back into the headrest and shut her eyes. She allowed herself to remember the moments of play in the sand, dancing in Steve's arms in the restaurant, sprawling with him in savage intimacy in the moonlight. When she had tortured herself enough with those memories, she thought about how it would be if she and Steve were married. They would wake up in each other's arms, shower together, share morning coffee, talk over the day's happenings while they ate supper, make love on Steve's ridiculous rug, sleep entwined in each other's arms. Then the telephone would ring, and she would have to leave and Steve would become angry. She would have to miss a dinner party that they had been planning for weeks, and Steve would become exasperated. She would come in late at night and he would demand supper. He would want to know why the house was such a mess. They would be at a party and she would have to leave. He would be angry and they would quarrel. He would get fed up and walk out the door. . . .

"*No!*" Barbara cried, sitting up in the seat. "Yes, oh, yes, I can do it. I can say no. Oh, Steve, don't you understand? I can be your lover, but not your wife." How she wished that she could be his wife! But she just couldn't. She looked out the windows at the Houston skyline. They were almost home.

They drove in silence to Barbara's condominium. The rain had stopped, but the sky was still overcast. The bright city lights reflected off the low clouds. Steve removed Barbara's cases from the trunk and placed them on the front step. Barbara got out of the car, holding her breath. She had stated her case. The ball was in his court.

Steve looked at Barbara in the light of the streetlamp. He cleared his throat. "Barbara, I don't want you for a lover," he said firmly. Barbara saw a look of deep pain in his eyes. "I want you for my wife, or I don't want you at all." He turned his head away from her and as she watched his face she knew he was fighting for control.

So Steve had made up his mind. And with his strong will he was not likely to change it. Barbara sucked in a sharp breath as pain tore through her midsection. "Then, I guess it's not at all," she said sadly. She walked toward the door, not looking back at him, let herself in and firmly shut the door behind her. She held back the tears until she was sure that Steve had driven off, then sat on her sofa and allowed her swimming eyes to flood her cheeks and drip onto her throw pillows. She knew that she had hurt him tonight, but what about her? Didn't her feelings count for anything? Why was Steve so adamant about getting married? Couldn't he understand why marriage was out of the question for her? Didn't he realize that marriage would destroy the love that they shared? Why was he destroying what could be a wonderful relationship for them both? Barbara wiped her cheeks and stared down at the coral ring. She ought to take it off now, but she didn't want to. Her thoughts returned to Steve. Were his

124

reasons moral ones? Was Steve opposed to affairs outside the marriage bond? He certainly had not impressed her as being that rigid. So what did they do now, throw it all away as Steve had said? Oh, why, Steve, why did you have to spoil it all? she screamed in her head. She sat on the sofa and wept for a while, then called her exchange to let them know that she was home and was taking calls again.

"How long has your husband been having these problems?" Barbara asked as she peered into Clyde Johnson's eye with her small flashlight.

"'Bout four or five hours," Maisie Johnson answered. The big black woman was normally very cheerful, but today she was worried about Clyde; and her usual wide smile was absent. "He started acting strange around lunchtime."

Barbara reached down with a pin and pricked Clyde's left arm. He did not respond in any way to her small assault. "Clyde, can you hear me?"

Clyde nodded and tried to speak, but his mouth would not seem to form the words.

Barbara shook her head slightly. "Maisie, I'm afraid that whatever it is that Clyde has suffered, it's beyond my range of expertise. I want him to see a neurologist as soon as possible this afternoon." She looked at Clyde critically. It was probably what the layman would call a stroke, but each stroke was unique in its cause and its effects, and it took the care of a specialist to treat a stroke victim properly. "Has Clyde been taking the medicine for his high blood pressure?"

"Yes, he sure has," Maisie reassured Barbara solemnly.

Barbara placed a quick call to Jerry Goldman, the neurologist whom she usually sent her patients to. "Jerry? Barbara Weimer here."

"And what can I do for the most popular heartthrob of the Houston Medical Society?" Jerry teased. He was an excellent neurologist but a hopeless flirt.

"Get serious, Jerry," Barbara snapped.

"Sorry, no sleep last night?" Jerry mocked.

No, and not for the last three nights before that, Barbara said to herself. Aloud, she said, "I have a patient here with numbness on the left side and garbled speech. Can you see him this afternoon?"

"Sure thing, beautiful. Send him on over. By the way, I saw your ex and the prim little missus the other night. Marsha's pregnant."

"Good for Marsha," Barbara said dryly. "Thanks, Jerry." Barbara hung up the telephone slowly. That was just what she needed to hear this afternoon. Marsha had succeeded once more where Barbara had failed. Curbing her ill temper, Barbara sent Clyde and Maisie to Jerry's downtown office, extracting a firm promise from Maisie that she would let Barbara know how Clyde fared. Sighing, Barbara walked into her office and kicked off her shoes. She picked up her list of telephone calls and propped her tired feet on her desk. So Marsha was pregnant. So what?

What indeed? It still hurts, Barbara thought, even though I don't love Wayne anymore. And Steve thinks he wants to marry Houston's number-one lousy wife! He ought to go talk to Wayne! Barbara's eyes swam with tears and she wiped them quickly lest Max or Sylvia see them on her face. Why had Steve forced her to give him up? The four days since they had driven home from the coast had seemed like a miserable eternity. She could never be a good wife and he knew it. So why wasn't he willing to settle for what she could offer him? Why was he so damned stubborn? Forcing herself to put Steve from her mind, she made her required telephone calls and kept her mind on those while she was talking, but thoughts of Steve and their tumultuous lovemaking intruded on her consciousness every time she put down the receiver.

Listlessly Barbara dragged herself out of the office and to the parking lot. There, parked beside her Corvette, sat the familiar

Jaguar. Barbara rubbed her tired eyes. It was just a cruel coincidence. Steve would not be parked beside her. Lower lip trembling, she made her way to the cars, becoming more confused by the second. This Jaguar was exactly like Steve's, down to the small scratch on the door. It had to be Steve's! She peered in puzzlement at the car, then jumped as she felt two strong arms creep around her and soft warm lips nuzzle her neck. "Steve," she breathed softly as she melted back into his arms. Tears of joy flooded her eyes and she wiped at them with the handkerchief he obligingly handed her.

"Miss me?" he taunted softly.

"Damn you, why did you stay away for so long?" Barbara cried, whirling around in his arms. She flung her arms around his neck, her eager embrace belying the anger in her voice. Joy flooded her entire being. He was back. But why? Was Steve agreeing to the affair that she wanted, or did he have another purpose in mind? She surveyed his face for some clue to his feelings. He looked tired, but though his eyes were tender, Barbara could not decipher his thoughts from his expression.

"I tried to stay away for a few days so that we could both think a little," Steve said. "I was going to stay away for a week, but I couldn't stand it," he admitted honestly.

"I couldn't stand it, either," Barbara agreed. For the moment it didn't matter why Steve had come to her. The important thing was that he had come, and that she could be with him again. With gentle fingers filled with love, she reached up and touched the scar on his forehead. "Where do you want to go?" she asked softly.

"I need to go back to the field office for a few minutes," he said. "Then out for a bite to eat and a talk. Okay by you?"

Barbara nodded, a joyous smile on her face, although she was still uncertain as to Steve's intentions. Squaring her shoulders unconsciously for the argument that was to come sometime in the evening, she took Steve's hand and followed him across the street to his office.

* * *

Steve carefully dodged the cars on the busy thoroughfare and led Barbara into the mobile office that was parked on one side of the building. He mounted the dusty stairs that led into the office and motioned to Barbara to come after him. Cautiously she followed him, grateful when a blast of cool air hit her face and soothed her flushed cheeks. She looked around the office with interest. It was pleasant enough but definitely functional, with linoleum floors that could be cleaned easily and no-nonsense furniture. The desks were littered with architectural blueprints and plastic coffee cups, and to one side a small portable television was showing the evening news. Steve pointed to the couch. "I won't be a minute," he said. "I want you to meet my architect. She's working late tonight."

She? Barbara thought as she sat down tiredly and tried to watch the news. I didn't realize his architect was a woman! We're invading all fields, Barbara thought with amusement.

Steve returned to the main room with a dark-haired woman behind him. Barbara stood smiling, but her smile turned to a look of astonishment that she quickly concealed when she realized that the woman who was with Steve was none other than Margo Langly. If Margo was surprised to meet Barbara, she did not show it. "Hello, Dr. Weimer," she said coolly.

"Miss Langly," Barbara said softly, extending her hand. "How are you?" Barbara surreptitiously peeked at Margo's figure. Seven or eight pounds were gone, and Margo's splendid build was becoming evident. Apparently Max had prescribed the pills. Sudden jealousy flared inside Barbara. This beautiful woman worked every day on an intimate basis with Steve, and she had to catch what little time she could have with him. She couldn't help wondering if Steve found Margo desirable.

"You two have met before?" Steve asked in surprise.

"In a manner of speaking," Margo said noncommittally. "I went to her once." Neither woman said more, but the tension between them was noticeable.

Steve turned to Margo and handed her a computer print-out. "See if you can do something about the design weaknesses here in these trusses," he said as he pointed to a column of figures. "I don't like the degree of uncertainty here."

"Neither do I," Margo admitted. "I'll get on it tonight."

"No big hurry," Steve said as he laid the print-out back on the desk. "Tomorrow is soon enough."

"I don't mind," Margo said as she stuffed the print-out in her briefcase. Steve turned his back to Margo and for an instant her face softened as she looked at his broad back, her eyes becoming gentle. My God, Barbara thought. Margo is in love with Steve. Barbara watched closely as Steve and Margo talked together for a few more minutes. He did not seem aware of Margo's feelings, nor did he seem to reciprocate them. If he did know that the woman was in love with him, he was not encouraging her in any way. Barbara was stunned for a moment. Was this why Margo had wanted the diet pills, to become beautiful so that Steve would notice her? If Barbara continued to refuse to marry Steve, would he turn to Margo for comfort? Barbara bit her lip in vexation. Even if Steve was not aware of Margo now, the woman's presence and love for him was a complication that Barbara had not anticipated and did not know how to handle.

Margo and Steve finished their business and Margo left, nodding to Barbara on the way out. Steve took Barbara's arm and together they negotiated the flight back through the traffic to her parking lot. "Your car or mine?" Barbara quipped lightly.

"Mine," Steve said firmly.

Steve drove to a small, quiet restaurant that specialized in seafood. What is he thinking? Barbara wondered as they made their selections from the menus. Steve kept the conversation on general topics, and unwilling to precipitate another argument over supper, Barbara followed his lead, her curiosity building as she ate her delicious shrimp plate and watched Steve wade through a variety platter. How did he intend to bring up the topic that was uppermost in their minds? Or did he intend to bring it up at all? Had he changed his mind about marrying her?

As Barbara finished her last morsel of shrimp, Steve pushed his plate away and folded his arms across the table. "Have you thought any more about marrying me?" he asked softly but with that hint of steel in his eyes.

"I've thought of little else," Barbara admitted slowly. "That is, when I've had time to think at all. I've had a busy week." She ran her fingers through her hair and looked at Steve with what she hoped was a calm expression. "I said all I had to say Sunday night. I can't consider another marriage, because I can't go through another divorce."

"Why are you so damned hardheaded?" Steve ground out. "With me there would be no divorce."

Barbara's beeper sounded, followed by the garbled message. "Sorry," she said, inwardly relieved at the reprieve. "I'll take that in the lobby."

It was Jerry Goldman on the telephone. "I wanted you to know that Clyde Johnson had a major stroke late this afternoon, after I had already admitted him to the hospital. Mrs. Johnson has been asking to talk to you. I don't think she trusts me." Jerry laughed faintly.

"That's what you get for making a pass at her," Barbara teased. "All right, I'll go down and have a talk with her."

"Thanks, beautiful," Jerry said as he hung up.

Barbara jumped as Steve took her elbow. "I have to go back to the hospital," she said ruefully.

"Okay," Steve said as he paid the bill, ushering her out the door. "Is it one of your patients?" he asked.

"Not exactly," Barbara explained when they reached the car. As they drove to the hospital in the heavy evening traffic, she went on. "I sent one of my patients to a neurologist this afternoon with some suspicious symptoms. Sure enough, he's had a massive stroke and his wife wants to talk to me. I don't think she trusts the neurologist."

Steve nodded. "I bet a lot of doctors wouldn't even bother to go down and talk to her," he mused thoughtfully.

"Maybe not," Barbara said firmly, "but I would."

"I wasn't criticizing you," Steve said softly. "I think that's great." But how great would he think it was if he was married to me? Barbara wondered.

Maisie Johnson was sitting forlornly in the ICU waiting room, tears streaking down her weathered face. "Oh, Dr. Weimer," she cried. "My Clyde is so sick and that other doctor, he doesn't know us and he said that I can't go in and see him! I want to see my Clyde!" The woman collapsed in a torrent of sobs.

Barbara reached out and patted the woman soothingly. "Maisie, I'm sure that in just a few minutes you'll get to go see Clyde. And Dr. Goldman is the best. I promise you. I wouldn't have sent Clyde to him if he hadn't been."

Maisie sniffed and wiped her eyes with the heel of her hand. "But he's so, well, so . . ." she trailed off uncertainly.

"Hi, beautiful," Jerry Goldman said as he sailed into the waiting room and put his arm around Barbara, kissing her soundly on the cheek. Barbara promised herself that one of these days she was going to shoot Jerry for his unprofessional behavior in front of a patient. Maisie's eyes widened, then a glimmer of a smile broke out on her face.

Barbara winked at Maisie. "Yes, he's definitely so-so," she whispered to Maisie as the little woman's face cleared.

"Mrs. Johnson, I want you to go and see your husband for just a few minutes. I'm sorry I couldn't let you see him earlier, but we were still running tests. He's had a massive stroke and it will be a long time before he recovers completely, but he will be all right. Now, dry those eyes, doll, and look pretty for your man."

"Yes, Dr. Goldman," Maisie said cheerfully, her earlier distress forgotten. She gathered up her purse and walked eagerly to the door of ICU.

"See there, beautiful, all it took was a few honeyed words from you, and the lady's happy again. How can I ever thank you?" Jerry sneaked his arm back around Barbara's waist.

"You can go home and kiss Rhonda and the kids for me," Barbara said wryly as she disentangled herself from his grasp. "Night, Jerry."

Steve was standing in the door, a thunderous expression on his face. "Who was that man who was all over you?" he asked tightly.

"The hospital octopus," Barbara said calmly, a small smile playing around her lips. "He feels the need to touch every female below the age of eighty. I hear he even hugs the department-store dummies." They walked together out into the cool night air.

"Then, why are you smiling?" Steve demanded imperiously.

"I'm smiling at you!" Barbara sputtered. "You're jealous!" Her merry laughter pealed out over the parking lot.

"You're damn right I'm jealous!" Steve thundered. "And I don't think it's one damned bit funny. You tell that man to quit pawing you."

Barbara laughed harder than ever, wiping the tears from her eyes. "I think you'd have to kill him to get him to stop," she admitted. She sobered slightly. "Steve, you have no need to be jealous of a character like Jerry. He is absolutely no competition for you. Absolutely none at all."

"And just who is competition for me?" Steve asked slowly.

"You have no competition," Barbara admitted softly.

Steve gathered her to him in a bone-shattering embrace. He just held her for a moment, then his lips met hers with devastating longing. Barbara held his face between her hands and returned his kiss hungrily, allowing the love she felt for Steve to flow from his body to hers. His hands fell to her waist, where he stroked the sensitive skin under her blouse until she moaned softly. They drew apart, and without speaking they drove back to the parking lot where Barbara's car was parked. The adrenaline was flowing in Barbara's veins, as she bit her lip in excitement. They would be together, loving each other as they had before, raising each other to new heights of ecstasy. She shivered a little in anticipation.

Steve pulled in beside her car and took Barbara into his arms. She clung to him, allowing her tongue to foray against his in a delightful skirmish, then gasping as he gathered one breast in his fingers and stroked it gently. "Your place or mine?" Barbara asked softly.

"Neither," Steve said as he nibbled the skin on her neck.

"Where, then?" Barbara murmured as she ran her fingers up Steve's arm.

"Nowhere," Steve said as he tickled Barbara's earlobe with his tongue.

Barbara pulled out of Steve's arms. "Nowhere?" she asked in bewilderment.

"That's right," Steve said calmly. "I don't want to have an affair with you. I want to marry you."

Barbara looked at him warily as she figured out what he was saying, then anger took over. "You won't have an affair with me because I won't marry you?" she asked in incredulous anger.

"That's right," Steve said firmly. "I can't have things my way, so I don't see why you should have them your way, either. No marriage, no affair."

"If you think you can blackmail me into marrying you by withholding sex, you are sadly mistaken," Barbara ground out furiously. "Women have been trying it for years."

"And a lot have been successful," Steve pointed out calmly.

"Sorry, Steve. It won't work with me," Barbara spat as she got out of his car. "I don't have to wait for you for sex."

Steve jumped out of his car and grabbed Barbara by the arm. She immediately regretted her rash statement as he looked into her eyes, his own furious. "Just what do you mean by that?" he demanded angrily.

Barbara's own anger melted in the face of his wrath. "I wouldn't do that, and you know it," she said softly. "But I'm not going to let you blackmail me into another horrible mistake by using sex. If you don't want an affair, then so be it. Your mind is made up. So is mine." She shook her head sadly. She had been right earlier. Steve had not changed his mind about marriage.

"We'll see," Steve said implacably as he took her into his arms for another bone-melting kiss. All too soon he let her go and she watched, again furious, as he drove away in the moonlight. She would not let him blackmail her into marriage!

But marriage did enter her mind more and more in the weeks that followed. Steve continued to see her several times a week, but they went neither to his home nor hers. He would kiss her and caress her with passion in the car, but he refused to share with her the intimacy of an affair. His stance angered Barbara, because she sorely missed the passion that they had shared, but as she got to know Steve better, it was not the sex that made her begin to think, oh, so reluctantly, of marrying him. It was the unfailing camaraderie that seemed to be natural between them, a bond that had nothing to do with sex, that made Barbara's treacherous heart rebel against her sensible head. They just seemed to belong together. Barbara repeatedly reminded herself of the fiasco with Wayne, but that episode receded farther and farther into her mind, to be replaced with images of Steve and what life with him could be. Barbara could feel herself softening in her attitude, and this scared her. She did not want to be hurt again, but less and less did the thought of being Steve's wife fill her with fear.

CHAPTER EIGHT

"Barbara, I have a favor to ask you," Steve said as he sipped his afterdinner coffee.

Barbara turned her gaze from the cool October twilight back to Steve's increasingly beloved face. In the weeks that they had been seeing each other, Barbara had never grown tired of the strong face with the broken nose. Openly revealing her love in a tender smile, she inclined her head. "What kind of favor do you need?" she asked curiously.

"I need to give a small party for some of the local contractors and their wives in a week or two," he explained. "I will have it catered, of course, and I can call the local maid service for the cleaning before and after, but I need a hostess for that night. If I choose a night that you're off, will you do it?"

"I-I don't know," Barbara stammered as she sipped her coffee. "You know I'm not very good at that sort of thing." Remembering the fiascos she had given for Wayne, she shook her head sadly. "No, Steve, I really don't think so."

"It wouldn't be like the parties you tried to give when you were married," Steve replied, accurately interpreting the reason for her refusal. "All the work would be done already. All I need is a hostess by my side to visit with my guests and make them feel at home. There wouldn't be that much to it, honestly."

"I really don't feel comfortable at that sort of thing," Barbara replied. Steve's face fell and instantly Barbara felt she had reacted unfairly. "So when do you want to give your party?" she asked hesitantly.

"Thursday night the second week of November," Steve said.

"I think if you and Max follow your usual pattern, he will have the beeper that evening."

Barbara did some swift mental calculations. "I am off that evening," she admitted. "How many people do you want to entertain, and how formal is the party?"

"About thirty, and you should dress up."

Barbara made a wry face. "Just what you need," she laughed ruefully. "Your ragamuffin doctor friend to grace your table."

"So buy a new dress," Steve replied. "If your clothes bother you that much, I'll go with you and help you pick something out. Look, Barbara, I don't know what that other man said or did to make you feel the way you do about yourself in a social situation, but you are a lovely and poised woman who wouldn't have any trouble holding a conversation with anyone whom I can think of. I wish you would give yourself a chance and be my hostess."

Barbara smiled involuntarily at Steve's compliments. After years of Wayne's disparaging remarks, a favorable opinion of her social skills was more than welcome. "But what if something should come up? Sometimes I'm called out even though Max does have the beeper."

"We'll deal with that if we have to," Steve replied firmly. "If you can't do it for me, I guess I could call Margo," he mused.

"I'll do it," Barbara said quickly, spurred by the thought of Margo taking her place at Steve's side. "If you'll help me find something to wear." She looked over at Steve and was exasperated to find an expression of amusement on his face. Had he known that Barbara was jealous of Margo and made the comment on purpose? Barbara gritted her teeth in irritation, but Steve only smiled blandly in reply. "Call Sylvia and have her put it on my calendar," she added, although it was extremely unlikely that she would forget the party.

"That's my girl," Steve said warmly as he sent a radiant smile Barbara's way. "Can you go shopping next Wednesday evening?" Barbara nodded. "We'll try the Galleria first." Steve's eyes became gentle. "I do appreciate the help."

"Certainly," Barbara replied as her beeper went off. She placed her call and discovered that she would be spending most of the evening delivering another baby. Kissing Steve good-bye in the parking lot, clinging to him as tightly as her strong arms would curl, she was tempted to scream out to him that she would marry him. God knows, I love him, she thought as she drove away, more than I ever loved Wayne, and the constant calls and the demands of medicine sure don't seem to bother him. But will he hurt me in the same way that Wayne did? Barbara shrugged her shoulders as she climbed out of her car and walked into the hospital. She just did not know the answer to that, and until she did she was sticking to her original decision not to marry.

Sylvia poked her head through the crack of the door of the small kitchen the next morning as Barbara was pouring her first cup of coffee. "There's a man on the telephone who says that I'm supposed to put a party on your calendar," she said hesitantly. "Do you know anything about it?"

Barbara nodded as Max strolled in and poured himself a cup. "That's Steve Sullivan and I did agree to be his hostess," she explained. "Put down the second Thursday in November."

"Is that the juicy dish that you rescued off the skyscraper?" Sylvia gushed. "I thought you didn't want to go out with him. What changed your mind?"

"Yeah, what did change your mind?" Max teased. "I thought you had sworn off parties."

Barbara blushed furiously. "I haven't sworn off parties or off men," she said firmly, wishing the telltale red of her cheeks would go away. "I've been seeing Steve for a few weeks and he asked me to be at a party as his hostess. That's all."

"That's something!" Sylvia mooned. "Can you imagine giving a party for that gorgeous dish? Can you imagine doing anything with that hunk?"

Imagining some of what she had done with Steve, Barbara reddened again. Sensing her embarrassment, Max laid his hand comfortingly on Barbara's arm. "Well, I think it's great. It's

137

about time you started going out again and having some fun. I was getting worried about you."

"Thanks," Barbara said quietly. "Now, everybody to work!" Max and Sylvia groaned as they filed out to handle their respective duties.

On the appointed Wednesday, Steve picked Barbara up at the office, and after they had demolished hamburgers from a fast-food restaurant, Steve drove to the Galleria, and once again they were walking through the huge doors into the mall. Barbara was unreasonably tense. She hated shopping for clothes. She knew that the clothes she chose were not quite right, but damned if she knew what she was doing wrong. When she was still at home, she had been content to let her fashion-conscious mother choose her entire wardrobe, but after that her shopping trips were few and far between, and usually not successful when she did go. Her wardrobe had been one of Wayne's pet peeves, and she was extremely reluctant to expose her lack of dress sense to another man. Stiffly she walked beside Steve, her hands clenched in her jacket pockets, until Steve reached into her pocket and felt the tight fist. "What is the matter?" he asked.

"I hate clothes shopping," Barbara admitted. "You're going to laugh at me."

"You hate shopping?" Steve asked, incredulous. "Why, shopping is fun!" Barbara looked at him doubtfully. He steered her in the direction of a small, expensive boutique. "Come on, and I'll show you what I mean."

A prune-faced saleswoman met them at the door. "May I help you?" she asked in a voice that was designed to chill.

Barbara started to back away, but Steve held her arm firmly. "This beautiful doctor has graciously consented to hostess a small gathering for me," he said in his best put-on rich drawl. "We'd like to see a few dresses in the three-hundred- to six-hundred-dollar range, please. It's just a little party."

"Of course, sir," the saleswoman replied graciously. "Madame-uh-doctor . . ."

"Dr. Weimer will do," Barbara replied, smothering a giggle. They swept into the store and followed the woman back to a rack of stunning fall party dresses in rich silks and taffetas. Finding the size nines, Barbara slowly examined one dress after another, becoming more bewildered by the minute. They were all beautiful. She turned to Steve, indecision stamped on her face. "Which one do you like?" she whispered.

"They're all nice," Steve replied. "Pick two or three that you like and go try them on."

Barbara quickly grabbed a red silk with a plunging neckline, a navy-blue sheath in taffeta, and a gauzy brown dress with a halter top. She retired to the dressing room and drew the red dress on slowly. As she struggled with the zipper, she heard a knock at the door. "It's Steve," he called softly.

Barbara opened the door and Steve came in with another dress over his arm. He hung up the dress and helped Barbara with the reluctant zipper. "Do you like it?" he asked as Barbara surveyed herself in the mirror.

"It makes me look like I belong to a slightly different profession," Barbara admitted as she surveyed her barely clad front in the mirror. Her breasts were exposed almost to the nipples, and the flaming red washed out her blond beauty. Even Barbara could see that this dress was not for her.

She took off the red dress and tried on the other two. The navy dress was stark and much too old for her, and the brown gauzy creation did terrible things to her skin tones. But she hadn't liked any of the other dresses on the rack. "I guess the brown one will have to do," Barbara said with a sigh.

"Before you make up your mind, why don't you try on this one?" Steve asked gently. He pulled the plastic cover off a simple mauve silk dress that Barbara had completely overlooked on the rack. It was cut simply and she had dismissed it as being unstylish. But if Steve wanted her to try it on, she would.

The minute she slipped into the dress, Barbara knew this was the one. It set off her slender curves to perfection, and the color

139

was a perfect compliment to her fair skin and hair. In the privacy of the dressing room she turned this way and that. She looked ravishing. There was no other word for it. "How did you know?" she asked incredulously.

Steve shrugged modestly. "I just did," he replied, leaving to take the discarded dresses back to the saleswoman. Gently Barbara took off the beautiful dress so as not to hurt it in any way. She was delighted. For once she was going to look as good as the rest of the women at the party.

She carried the dress to the cash register. As the woman rang up the sale, Barbara fumbled around in her purse. Suddenly strong fingers gripped her arm. "I'll buy you the dress," Steve said softly.

"That's all right," Barbara said absently as she fished out her checkbook. "I can afford it."

"I said I'd buy it," Steve replied. "That dress was almost five hundred dollars!" Barbara ignored him and flipped open her checkbook.

Without meaning to, Steve glanced over her shoulder and gasped when he saw her bank balance. "On second thought, I'll let you pay for the dress," he muttered.

"I told you I could afford it," Barbara said calmly.

The next day Barbara slipped out at noon and shopped doggedly until she had found a pair of lizard sandals that would set off her dress to perfection. Barbara paid for her purchase and drove back to the office, singing with the car radio. I'm really looking forward to Steve's party, she thought with astonishment. She hadn't looked forward to a party in years.

Steve was sitting on the hood of her car as he usually did on Friday afternoons, but today he was not alone. Beside him sat a husky boy with sun-streaked brown hair and a lively smile. Steve and the boy jumped off the hood as Barbara approached the car. She extended her hand and the boy took it readily. "I'm Barbara Weimer," she said, smiling at the boy warmly.

"I'm Steve, but everyone calls me Scooter," he piped up. "Do I call you Dr. Weimer?"

"I like Barbara better." She smiled softly. Barbara's insides melted for this darling boy. He was so much like Steve. He was neatly dressed in rather expensive clothing, but had that all-boy aura that suggested that he was thoroughly at home on a sandlot or a set of monkey bars. He looked at her with Steve's direct gaze and his face split into a wide smile.

"Dad said you have a beeper that goes off all the time," he volunteered. "Will it go off for us tonight?"

"Probably," Barbara said wryly as Steve reached forward and took her into his arms. Their kiss and embrace was more restrained than usual in deference to Scooter, but the longing was there—subdued, but definitely present. Barbara wondered again if she was wrong in not wanting to marry Steve. What if he was right? What if a marriage between them could survive?

Steve took them all back to Lucy's and, amazed, Barbara watched Scooter put away as much food as Steve. The young boy was a perfectly charming individual and Barbara took to him instantly. Steve sat back and let Barbara and Scooter carry the conversation, smiling smugly when it became obvious that they were becoming fast friends. After supper Steve dropped Scooter off at his mother's house, promising him that Barbara's beeper would go off the next time they were together. As Scooter waved from the door and shut it behind him, Barbara laughed softly. "Imagine anyone wanting my beeper to go off," she said. "On the one night it would have been welcome, it's as silent as a sleeping baby." At that moment the beeper sounded.

"Baby just woke up," Steve said dryly.

Steve stopped at the corner drive-in and Barbara made her call. She did not have to go back to the hospital, so she and Steve drove around for a while, just enjoying being together. "Scooter is wonderful," Barbara volunteered.

"Thank you," Steve said with obvious pride. "I could tell that he likes you, too."

"How much did you tell him about me?" Barbara asked curiously.

"Fishing?" Steve teased. "I told him that you were a very special lady and that I hope you will marry me soon."

"Steve," Barbara said warningly.

"Let's not go into that tonight," Steve replied firmly. "Are you ready for my party?"

"You know, I'm actually looking forward to it," Barbara mused. "I never thought after all those fiascos with Wayne that I would say that."

"Well, there's no way this one will be a fiasco," Steve said reassuringly.

"I hope you're right." Barbara sighed. "I used to get called away in the middle of them."

"Well, we won't have that problem if Max has the beeper that night. Now, I think I'll get you back to your car so you can go to bed and sleep," Steve said blandly.

"By all means, I do need the rest," Barbara returned acidly. She wanted to go to bed, all right, but not alone and not to sleep! As she drove home and again later as she sat on her couch sipping a glass of wine, marriage to Steve once again invaded her thoughts. God knows, we love each other, she thought. Their feelings for each other were plain every time they embraced. So what's stopping me? Why am I letting old hurts get in the way of a glorious future with Steve? Barbara ran her fingers through her hair and imagined what married life with Steve would be like. Warm chills shook her body as she remembered the explosive passion they had shared as lovers. And he doesn't seem to resent the long hours or the beeper, she mused. It doesn't seem to bother him at all.

Barbara sat on her couch until almost dawn. She was depriving herself of much-needed sleep, but she did not care. Finally she was convinced that things would work out all right. "I'll do it!" she said out loud. She would take the plunge and marry Steve. She would put aside all the prejudice that she had against marriage and this time it would work. With Steve it had to. She was suddenly giddy with excitement. She was going to get married. She was going to marry the man she loved. She got up and danced around the room, and picked up the telephone receiver to call Steve and tell him that he had won. But she placed the receiver in the cradle and padded to the bedroom instead. No, to call Steve and accept his proposal over the telephone was not the best way to handle this. She would wait until they had a more romantic place and time. Barbara thought a moment. Of course! She would tell him Thursday night after the party, and by Friday she would be back in Steve's arms for the whole night. Suddenly giddy with fatigue, Barbara fell across her bed and slept soundly until her alarm went off at nine and she had to get up and make rounds.

Barbara hummed softly as she bounded up the steps to the back door of the office. A cool rain blew in her face, but as far as she was concerned, it was May and the sun was shining. Tonight was Steve's party, and after the party she would tell Steve that she would marry him. Smiling secretively, Barbara shed her coat and pulled on her white jacket. She and Max always closed their office on Thursday afternoon, and Barbara had even made an appointment at a beauty salon for the works, a treat that she had not allowed herself in years. Greeting Sylvia cheerfully, Barbara grabbed a cup of coffee and sailed into her morning appointments with vigor, enjoying her work more than usual because she was deliciously anticipating the evening to come. Max and Sylvia winked at each other and grinned behind Barbara's back. It was about time Barbara did something besides work!

At precisely twelve noon Barbara bade her last patient goodbye and headed to her office to make her list of telephone calls. She was about halfway through the calls when Max stuck his head through the door, a frightened expression on his face.

"Barbara, Eileen just called. Mary fell off the monkey bars at school and broke her arm. I have to meet them in the emergency room. Could you possibly take the beeper for an hour or two?"

Barbara heaved a sigh of relief. Her beauty salon appointment was not until three. "All right," she agreed. "But just for an hour or two."

Max called the exchange and gave them instructions to transfer all calls to Barbara, then ran out the back door. Barbara chided herself for being put out. Mary was Max's child, for heaven's sake. He had to be with her. Gathering up her purse and the dratted beeper, Barbara headed for home and made herself a light lunch, knowing that she would be having a substantial meal later. Very carefully she pressed the silk dress and laid it out on her bed so that she could slip into it at the last minute. The beeper had sounded twice by two, and although both of those problems could be handled by telephone, Barbara began to get a little anxious. Max was supposed to be taking calls again by now, but he had not notified the exchange to transfer the calls back to him. Irritated, Barbara called the hospital and asked to speak to Max.

After long minutes had ticked away, Barbara's call was put through to the OR waiting room. Eileen Vaughan answered the telephone. "May I speak to Max?" Barbara asked tersely.

"Max is in the OR," Eileen said in a voice that was not quite steady. "Mary's arm had to be operated on, and the surgeon that Max called invited him to sit in on the operation." Barbara nodded, ashamed of her previous irritation. The surgeon had extended the usual courtesy to another professional, and Max was well within his responsibilities as a parent to observe the surgery. "Max said to tell you that as soon as he could, he would get back to the beeper."

"Tell him thanks," Barbara mumbled. "And I sure hope Mary is all right."

"Thanks," Eileen said as she hung up.

Barbara sighed. Maybe if she was lucky, there would be no more calls until after she had been to the beauty salon. As though

144

to mock her very thoughts, the beeper went off just as Barbara walked in the door of the salon, summoning her to the hospital to treat the victims of an automobile accident.

It was well after five by the time Barbara was able to leave the hospital. None of the accident victims was seriously injured, but by the time she had ordered and read X rays and sewed up their cuts and set one simple fracture, it was too late to go back to the salon. Fuming, she slammed her car into gear and drove home as fast as she could in the teeming Houston traffic. She was not due at Steve's until seven thirty, so she still had plenty of time to make herself presentable, provided the beeper did not go off. She stretched out in a leisurely bath and soaked away the frustration of the missed beauty-salon appointment. She washed her hair and dried it straight this time, intending to wind it into a knot on top of her head. Very carefully she pulled on her lacy underwear and pantyhose and sat down to make up her face. She had outlined and shadowed her eyes in a delicate shade of mauve and coated them with mascara when her telephone rang.

Barbara heaved a sigh of relief. That would be Max, telling her that he would take all the calls from now on. Instead it was their exchange. They had received a call from a patient and they could not reach Dr. Vaughan. Was she still taking calls?

Cursing Max loudly, much to the shock of the operator, Barbara agreed to take the call. The exchange gave her the telephone number of Phil Harris. Probably nothing, Barbara thought optimistically as she dialed the number. She would take this call and then she would track Max down, physically if she had to. Jeannie Harris answered the telephone. "Dr. Weimer here," Barbara said crisply.

"I hate to bother you," Jeannie said hesitantly. "In fact Phil said not to call. But I'm worried. He's been having pains in his chest all afternoon and he looks a little funny."

"Funny like how?" Barbara asked quickly.

"Sort of gray-like," Jeannie replied.

Oh, no, Barbara thought with dread. That didn't sound good.

"Jeannie, you put Phil in the car and get him to the emergency room right away. I'll meet you there."

"Yes, Dr. Weimer," Jeannie replied, open fear in her voice.

"Now, Jeannie, don't get upset or expect the worst. Just bring Phil in. It's probably nothing," Barbara assured her. Replacing the receiver in the cradle, she said aloud, "I hope to God it isn't what I think it is." She raced into a pair of jeans and threw on a clean blouse, then ran to the car and plunged back into the heavy traffic, leaving all thoughts of a party behind her with the dress on the bed.

Oh, hell, Barbara thought sickly as she strode into the emergency room cubicle and looked at Phil's ashen face. He was having a heart attack. His blood pressure was so low that Barbara had trouble getting a reading. He was dazed and moaning with pain, clutching at his chest and his arm. Picking up the stethoscope, Barbara placed it against Phil's chest and found the predicted irregular heartbeat. She snapped an order for an EKG and snatched the telephone from the cradle, dialing the number she had memorized from past episodes like this one. "Get me Dr. Stattler," she snapped in a businesslike voice. Harold Stattler was the best cardiologist in Houston, and she needed his help.

"Dr. Weimer, Dr. Stattler is tied up on another case over at Ben Taub," the exchange operator volunteered. "And his partner is out of town on business. I'm sorry."

Barbara thanked the operator, swearing only after she had hung up the receiver. Although she was as well trained as the next doctor, she never felt comfortable with a heart attack. But she had handled them alone before and her patients had survived, and she would handle this one. Barbara nodded to the EKG technician, who flipped the switch and made a few adjustments. Then the machine began to print out a pattern that made Barbara groan inwardly. It revealed that Phil Harris had suffered a major heart attack.

Barbara immediately ordered the setting up of an IV with medication and fluids. She instructed a nurse to go get Jeannie

Harris, and Barbara quietly explained the situation to her. Barbara would not leave Phil until he was stable or another doctor came to release her. Once the IV was set up, Barbara asked Jeannie to wait in the hall, and Barbara watched Phil for any signs of improvement.

Suddenly the EKG started to blip and the alarm sounded, and at that precise moment Phil passed out. Oh, no, Barbara thought, the powerful muscles of the lower part of the heart had gone into a frenzied, irregular beat. "More medication," Barbara ordered, shooting the lifesaving fluid into Phil's body. Cold fear raced down her spine as she watched for Phil's reaction to the medication. Every nurse and technician in the room held her breath along with Barbara. "Come on, Phil!" Barbara whispered. "You can do it!"

Mercifully Phil began to respond. His heartbeat steadied some and his eyelids flickered open. "This . . . is . . . hell," he whispered with labored breath.

"I know," Barbara said gently. "Phil, I want you to conserve your strength for me. No more talking, just relax as much as you can. All right?" Phil nodded.

The next two hours were an eternity to Barbara and the entire cardiac team. As the doctor in charge Barbara stayed glued to Phil's bedside, periodically wiping nervous sweat from her brow as she rode the tide with Phil. Despite the fact that Barbara and the team had each been through this many times before, the atmosphere was thick with tension. They were literally battling for a man's life, and if they lost so would he.

Barbara pumped more medication into Phil but this time the sought-after slowing of the heartbeats did not occur, and Phil did not regain consciousness. "Damn!" Barbara snapped at nobody in particular. She bit her lip in frustration. "Give me the shocks," she ordered.

The nurse handed Barbara the electroshock paddles. Barbara positioned them on Phil's chest and shocked him once, hard, and thankfully his heart returned to a more normal beat. Barbara closed her eyes for a moment in gratitude. Another thirty minutes passed, Phil's condition remained the same, and the atmosphere in the room was tense. Barbara's head was pounding, but she did not dare walk out of the room to get medication for herself. She gritted her teeth and willed the pain to go away.

The sudden bleep of the EKG and the horrible reading that it produced caused Barbara to forget her own headache. Phil's heart had stopped completely! Swearing under her breath, Barbara administered more medication, and without waiting to see if that was effective, immediately gave him another powerful electroshock. His heart began to beat irregularly for about three minutes and went into complete arrest again. Barbara shocked him again and administered more of the now ineffective medication. Phil responded again, and this time his heart beat for about ten minutes.

Come on, Phil, I know you can do it, Barbara said silently. You have to. You're too damn young for this insanity. Even as Barbara thought this, Phil's heart arrested again. In vain she tried the shocks, but they, too, had become useless. "We're going to CPR," Barbara ordered, aware that this was her last chance to save Phil.

They worked for at least thirty minutes, long enough for Barbara's arms to become totally exhausted and the nurse to become breathless. Finally Barbara stopped pumping Phil's chest and motioned for the nurse to quit mouth-to-mouth. "He's gone," Barbara said flatly. They had failed, and Phil was dead. The rest of the team filed out except the EKG technician, who started unhooking the electrodes from Phil's body. Barbara stood looking down at Phil Harris. This morning he had been the man with everything. Tonight he was dead. She had not been able to save him.

Barbara stared down at Phil, handsome even in death. Oh, God, Phil, why did I have to lose you? Phil, of all people, who had so much to live for. He had not just been a patient. He had been an admired friend. Barbara felt tears course down her

148

cheeks and wiped them away. "Phil, I'm sorry." She sobbed out loud. "I'm going to miss you." And she would grieve for this man and wonder for months, years, maybe, if she had made one wrong decision that had made the difference.

Drained and exhausted, Barbara realized that she still had Jeannie and the kids to talk to. And that is going to be the hardest part of this whole tragedy, she thought brokenly. She wiped her eyes and reached out and covered Phil's body with a sheet, then walked out into the corridor, shutting the door behind her.

Jeannie and the children were sitting in the waiting room at the end of the hall, each one holding hands with their mother. Beside Marilyn sat a nice-looking young man in his early twenties. When Marilyn saw the look on Barbara's face, she started to weep softly and the young man put his arms around her. Jeannie sat numbly, stunned beyond tears. "He didn't make it, did he?" she asked dazedly.

"I'm so sorry," Barbara whispered, tears glistening in her eyes. "We did everything we could to save him."

"Thank you for everything," Mike spoke up, tears unashamedly streaking down his face. "Dad thought the world of you."

"I thought the world of him, too," Barbara replied.

"Thank you again," Jeannie whispered as her son led the family away.

Barbara unlocked the front door to her apartment and shuffled wearily inside, then pushed it shut behind her. She threw her purse and keys onto the counter and, walking straight to the refrigerator, pulled out a cool bottle of wine and poured herself a generous glass. Normally Barbara was most restrained in her use of alcohol, but tonight she needed a drink. She sat down on the couch forlornly and sipped her wine, dissecting the evening moment by moment, trying in vain to figure out if or when she had done the wrong thing. Had she used the shocks too soon?

149

Not soon enough? Too much medication? Not enough soon enough? Or would anything she could have done made any difference? Wearily she ran her hand across her forehead and down her hair. She simply did not know the answer to those questions, and she never would. She sighed and drank her wine. She would finish the glass, go to bed, and try to sleep a little.

Barbara's doorbell sounded twice in succession. Dragging herself from the couch, Barbara groaned at the late hour and hoped whoever it was would not keep her long. Peeking out the peephole, she could barely make out Steve standing in the dim light of the hallway. Barbara backed away from the door and switched on the light. She opened the door with a tired "hello" on her lips, but the greeting froze in her mouth at the furious expression on Steve's face as he pushed his way into her front hall.

"Where the hell have you been?" he snapped. "You were supposed to be at my party, remember?"

Barbara stared at him, dumbfounded. She swallowed. "I'm sorry, Steve," she murmured. "I got tied up. . . ."

"You got tied up?" he asked incredulously. "You knew you were supposed to be at my place by seven, and it's nearly midnight. Where the hell have you been?"

Barbara's incredulity at Steve's outburst faded a little, giving way to anger. "I was at the hospital," she said through tight lips.

"Where else would you be?" Steve gibed. "You were supposed to be free this evening, and damn it, I was counting on you."

So was someone else, she thought. "I said that I was sorry," she replied tersely. "It simply couldn't be helped."

"Well, you were supposed to see that you were free," Steve said angrily. "How do you think I felt, no hostess, no telephone call, and forty guests, including some of the biggest businessmen in Houston? I felt pretty embarrassed, that's how I felt! And you think an 'I'm sorry, it couldn't be helped' will make it all right!"

"If you recall, I didn't particularly want to serve as your hostess in the first place," Barbara ground out, her anger punctuating her headache. "You talked me into it, remember?"

"Because I thought you would do your best to be there. Damn it, Barbara, I didn't ask you to cook the damn dinner or clean the house. I just asked you to be there. Was that so hard? I didn't think so. But no, you don't make arrangements for another doctor to cover for you, and then you get yourself held up and don't even bother to call! That's pretty damned inconsiderate, if you ask me. I may have lost several accounts, thanks to you."

"Well, you aren't the only one who lost something tonight," Barbara yelled at him, completely furious now and not bothering to hide it. "Phil Harris and I lost something a hell of a lot more important than a couple of damned accounts!" Her voice wobbled dangerously, but Steve was too caught up in his own anger to notice.

"Who the hell is Phil Harris and what does he have to do with the fact that you ducked out on my party?" Steve demanded angrily. "Why were you even taking calls, anyway?"

Barbara choked as she began to cry. "All right, if you want to know the whole story, you're gonna," she sobbed as she advanced on Steve, her finger poking into his chest, backing him down the hall as she talked. "I had every intention of going to your party. Stupid me, I bought shoes to go with the damned dress and even made an appointment at the beauty shop." Tears ran down her cheeks and she dashed them away angrily. "I was even looking forward to it."

Steve stumbled over the threshold of her bedroom. His eyes widened as he took in the mauve silk dress, carefully laid out across the bed, and the shoe box beside it. He eyed her warily. "So what happened?" he asked tensely.

Barbara sniffed and rubbed her eyes with the back of her hand. "Mary Vaughan fell off the monkey bars at school and broke her arm. Max had to go to the hospital and I had to take the beeper. I missed the beauty shop appointment, as you might have guessed, because I had to put a couple of reckless drivers back together. But I was still going to make it to your party. I was trying to get ready to go. But Max had not started taking calls when Jeannie Harris called. Her husband was having a heart attack."

Barbara raised her head and looked Steve straight in the eye, streaked mascara running down her cheeks. "Frankly, at that point I forgot all about your party, which is probably a good thing, because if I had been worrying about it I wouldn't have been able to function. I tried to call in a cardiologist but couldn't get one. I had to take care of Phil Harris by myself. I got home all of fifteen minutes ago."

Steve whistled through his teeth. "So you forgot about the party completely," he said flatly. "You couldn't even bother to call me."

"There's no 'bother' to it," Barbara spat at him. "You just don't walk out on a heart attack, even to go to the bathroom. What was I supposed to say, 'Sorry, Phil, I have to go call my boyfriend before I can get your heart beating again'? Oh, hell, Steve, go home. I'm too tired to fight with you tonight." She squared her shoulders and walked back to the living room.

Steve followed her slowly. "So your patient made you forget the party entirely," he said quietly. Suddenly his fist came down on the end table. "Damn it, Barbara, how do you think that makes me feel?"

"Well, how do you think I feel?" Barbara retaliated brokenly. "I spent nearly three hours with a man, desperately trying to save his life. I failed. Got that? A forty-four-year-old husband and father is dead tonight, and I'll never know if I did something wrong and caused that death. I fought for three hours and I failed, and I had to go tell his wife and kids that he was gone. And then I have to listen to you rant and rave about your party! Frankly, Wayne, your party was not that important tonight."

"Wayne?" Steve repeated, stunned. He looked at her in horror. "You called me 'Wayne.' "

Barbara shook her head wearily. "It's no wonder," she said

softly. "Wayne and I had this fight every other week." She picked up her wineglass and gulped its remaining contents, then walked to the kitchen and filled it again. She wandered back to the living room and sat down, tucking one leg under her while Steve eyed her critically. "Steve, up until now I don't think you realized the extent to which my profession dominates my private life. Sure, you've gone along with the interruptions and put up with the long hours and the beeper because it was new to you and it hadn't really affected you personally. But tonight I had to let you down because of my professional obligation. I had to put my patient first, and you blew up. It bothered you. You knew I was at the hospital, I was bound to be, and you were jealous."

"I was not jealous!" Steve snapped irately. "I was hacked off, angry at your lack of consideration—what I thought was your lack of consideration," he amended hastily as Barbara's head shot up.

"So without so much as one question, you tear me apart with your tongue just like Wayne used to do," Barbara said sarcastically. "No, on second thought, you're better at it than he was."

"That shot was cheap and uncalled-for," Steve ground out.

"Yes, it was," Barbara admitted. "But it was nevertheless true."

Steve took a deep breath and exhaled it slowly, willing the anger to leave him. "Barbara, I'm sorry. I really am. I'm sorry I yelled at you and I'm sorry your patient died. But that damn beeper and all the interruptions have really started getting to me. Tonight I blew."

Barbara looked at him sadly, fresh tears welling in her eyes. "And you honestly think you want to marry me?" she asked him softly.

"I do!" Steve insisted.

Barbara shook her head. "And to think that tonight I was going to tell you that I'd changed my mind," she said almost to herself, "that I would marry you." She looked at Steve and wiped her eyes. "Maybe it's just as well," she said softly. "It would never have worked."

"Barbara, no!" Steve cried desperately. "You can't mean that!" He sat down beside her and shook her lightly. "You don't mean that!"

Barbara shook her head sadly. "You just proved in the worst possible way that marriage is out of the question, Steve. I had to put a man's life first tonight. I *had* to! And you just didn't understand." Barbara sniffed loudly and reached for a tissue. "Look, it's not all your fault. A husband has a right to be his wife's first priority on a night like tonight, and I could never give you that."

Steve paled beneath his tan. "If you say so," he said when he realized that she had said all she had to say. He got up and left, slamming the door behind him.

And so where does that leave me? Barbara asked herself as she finished the second glass of wine. Steve's performance tonight proved that, for all his talk, marriage to him would be no different from what marriage to Wayne had been. Choking on sobs, Barbara stared out at the lights of Houston, watching them shimmer and sparkle from behind her tears. And she loved Steve! She had been so happy that she had decided to marry him. You are a fool, she told herself. You should have known that it would never work. She wiped tears from her cheeks and beat the couch with her fist. You'd better be glad you found out before the wedding this time, she chided herself. But I thought he was different, she wailed inwardly, I thought my career didn't bother him. Steve's admission that it did had been a stinging blow. And his rage at her absence from his party, whether or not it was justified, had absolutely stunned her. I misjudged him, she thought, and I set myself up for just this kind of disappointment. Was it so wrong for her to want love?

Hold on, girl, she reminded herself. You never said that love was out, only marriage. But with Steve the two were one and the

154

same. To him love meant marriage and he wasn't willing to settle for less. Barbara wiped her eyes and stumbled to her bedroom, where the sight of the silk dress on her bed brought a fresh round of sobs. She hung the dress in the closet, careful not to spot it with her tears. She crawled into bed, and as the wine took effect and her eyes closed in sleep, her last thought was that she and Steve had reached a total stalemate.

CHAPTER NINE

Barbara turned up the collar of her gray wool coat and walked slowly down the steps of the funeral home. The first norther of the season had blown away the rain, and bright autumn sunlight bounced off the white concrete sidewalks and driveway. The service for Phil had been packed. He had been one of the best-loved businessmen in Houston, and it seemed as though half of the business community had come to pay their respects. Barbara watched dully as the pallbearers carried Phil's casket to the waiting hearse. He was to be buried in his hometown of Lockhart, so there would be no graveside ceremony today.

Slowly Barbara walked down the driveway to the parking lot. She dreaded going home. For once she wished that it had been her weekend with the beeper. The constant interruptions would have taken her mind off last Thursday night, the disastrous evening that she had not been able to put out of her mind. If she was not thinking about Phil, she was thinking about Steve. Sighing, she walked across the parking lot and saw a tall, brown-haired man standing beside her car. Steve! What was he doing here?

Cautiously, Barbara walked to her car, unsure whether she was glad to see Steve or not. Their bitter argument Thursday night had left her hurting and angry, and frankly she would have preferred a few more days to deal with her turbulent emotions before seeing him. But he was here, and she would make the best of it.

Barbara looked at Steve warily, her conflicting emotions clearly visible in her face. Steve reached out and touched the deep

156

circle under one eye, wincing when she flinched away. "I guess I helped put that there," he said quietly.

"Yes, you did," Barbara replied frankly. "How did you know I was here?"

"Max said you'd probably be here," he replied. Steve looked distinctly uneasy. "Barbara, I know what I did last Thursday was unforgivable, and I wouldn't blame you if you never spoke to me again. But if you will forgive me long enough to talk to me, I'd like to take you out for a cup of coffee."

Barbara nodded, soothed a little by his apology. "Of course I'll forgive you," she said quietly. "I love you."

"Oh, Barbara, I love you," Steve said as he drew her gently into his arms and held her comfortingly. Barbara clung to him desperately, not with passion but with simple need. Then Steve suggested a small coffee shop a few blocks away. Soon they were sitting together in a small, cozy booth. Steve handed Barbara a menu. "Go ahead and eat something," he suggested. "You look like you need it."

At first Barbara was reluctant, but she finally settled on a simple hamburger. They sat silently while the waitress filled their coffee cups with the steaming brew, neither willing to make small talk. Finally, as the waitress walked away, Steve reached out and touched the coral ring on Barbara's middle finger. "You weren't angry enough with me to take it off," he commented. "I wondered if you would."

Barbara shook her head. "No, I'm still wearing it," she said softly.

Steve smiled slightly. "I'd like you to take me back," he said simply. "You said you were willing to have an affair with me. Are you still willing?"

Barbara looked at Steve shrewdly. Did he mean it, or did he have something up his sleeve?

"I know you probably don't believe it, but I do want the affair," Steve said quietly. "I'm still not convinced that it will work, but you sure as hell won't marry me now, so we'll do it your way, if you'll still have me."

A glaze of tears covered Barbara's eyes. "Of course I'll still have you," she said softly. She was surprised and touched by Steve's humility. "And I honestly think the affair will work out just fine, you'll see." The tears left her eyes and she felt herself growing elated because she had not lost him.

"Thanks," Steve said softly, unclenching his fists under the table. The waitress brought Barbara's hamburger and, hungry for the first time in days, she wolfed it down and finished her coffee. She looked over at Steve with a distinctly wicked expression on her face, to meet his expression of such blatant sensuality that it took her breath away.

"I don't have the beeper," she said softly. "Your place or mine?"

"Mine," Steve replied as he tossed a ten-dollar bill on the table and took Barbara's hand. "It's exactly one point two miles closer!" Eagerly they ran out of the restaurant to their waiting cars.

"Dr. Weimer, it's Mr. Sullivan on the telephone," Sylvia said as she poked her head into the examining room. "Can you take the call?"

"Sure," Barbara replied as she made a note on the chart she was holding. In truth she had an office full of patients and more on the way, but she had not talked to Steve for four days, and she desperately wanted to hear the sound of his voice. She popped into her office and picked up the extension. "Steve? How are you?" she asked anxiously.

"Tired," Steve replied frankly. "Look, Barbara, I'm on the run. I've been called back to Mexico on that damned project down there. I guess tonight's shot."

"Oh, no!" Barbara cried before she could stop herself. Almost beside herself with disappointment, she spoke out impulsively. "Do you have to go?" She knew that she sounded plaintive, but she couldn't help it.

'Yes; I have to go," Steve replied acidly. "I have a career, too, you know."

"Sorry," Barbara mumbled, instantly contrite. "Do you know when you'll be back?"

"No," Steve said shortly. "As soon as I can. Have to go now. Bye."

He forgot to tell me he loves me, Barbara thought forlornly as she hung up the receiver. Damn! she thought as she slapped her desk with her palm. This was the first free evening they had had in nearly two weeks, and Steve had to be out of town.

You, know, Barbara, this affair isn't turning out to be what you thought it would, she admitted to herself as she drove home in the December cold. The traffic was even worse than usual, with everyone out doing Christmas shopping. What should I get Steve? she wondered. A new coat? Something for his house? That new mood-elevating drug that's supposed to be so good? His mood lately could sure use elevating.

Barbara stuck a TV dinner in the stove and showered while it cooked. She pulled on an old flannel robe and slippers and took her dinner out of the stove. The enchilada plate was passable, and Barbara, not really caring about what she was eating, tried to figure out what was going wrong with the affair that she had wanted so badly.

They had resumed it beautifully enough. Steve had taken her back to his home, and they had made love all afternoon and fixed sandwiches together for supper. Barbara had spent the night in Steve's arms, getting up early and rushing home for a shower and change before going to work. Steve had met her for supper that evening, and mercifully the beeper left them alone for another night of bliss. But since then it seemed as though the two simply could not arrange enough time to be together. If Barbara had the beeper, Steve ended up spending the evening at the hospital with her, or she had to call him at the last minute and cancel. If she was free, he had a call from one of his clients and had to spend the evening with him, or something went wrong on one of the

159

jobsites and he and Margo were bent over their huge worktable until midnight. Steve's temper had flared with her more than once, and Barbara had failed to bite back a few comments of her own. On the few nights they had managed to have together, the passion that they shared was as fulfilling as ever, but Barbara wondered if those rare moments shared were enough to offset the pressures that were beginning to erode the relationship.

Barbara dumped her empty plate in the trash and wandered over to the window, to stare out into the darkness while her mind raced with all the unanswered questions that had been plaguing her for days. She desperately hoped she'd find a solution—and soon, because this affair had to work. It just had to.

Steve called her a week later from the airport. "I'm back," he said quietly as Barbara made notes on the last chart of the day.

Relief and gladness flooded through Barbara. Although she had received a postcard from Steve, she had missed him unbearably. "Do you want me to pick you up in an hour or so?" she asked eagerly. "I only have a few calls."

"Yeah, that would be nice," Steve replied. "I'll wait for you in the bar. And Barbara," he added slowly.

"Yes?" she asked hesitantly.

"I missed you like hell!"

Steve was perched on a barstool drinking a beer when Barbara slipped into the bar. She sat down on the stool beside him and kissed his cheek gently. He reached out and enfolded her in a huge bear-hug. Breathless, Barbara clung to him desperately, wanting to draw him into her very soul. He kissed her gently on her lips and released her reluctantly. "Would you like a drink?" he asked.

"I'll join you in a beer," Barbara replied.

They talked of his trip and Steve told her all about the differences in Mexican construction regulations. She in turn told him a few of the funny things that had happened in the office that week. As they talked, warm and loving with each other, Barbara heaved a sigh of relief. They weren't snarling at each other as they had been for the last few weeks. Maybe it was going to be all right after all. As she finished her last swallow of beer, Steve turned to her and leered wickedly. "Your place or mine?" he whispered.

"It doesn't matter—damn!" Barbara exclaimed as the beeper went off.

Steve's face fell. "Go make your call," he said softly. Disgusted, Barbara went in search of a telephone. Marianne Harper was in labor with her first baby, so it would be several hours before the baby was born, but the evening was gone. Hesitant, Barbara turned to Steve and explained the problem. Nodding tiredly, he told her to take him on home. "Will you come by afterward?" he asked. "Even if it's only for a little while."

Barbara did some swift mental arithmetic. "We're talking about one or two in the morning," she said. "Are you sure?"

"No, don't come," Steve replied quietly as he climbed into her car. "You have to get up and go to work tomorrow, and so do I."

"I'm sorry," Barbara said softly. Almost in tears, she slammed the Corvette into gear and roared out of the airport parking lot. She drove to Steve's house and parked in front. "Let me call the hospital and see how Marianne's doing," she volunteered. "If she hasn't dilated that much, maybe I could come in for a little while." Steve smiled broadly and together they went into his house. Barbara called the hospital, but as she had feared, Marianne was making good progress and she would need Barbara soon. "I'm sorry," she said as she turned to Steve. "She's further along than I thought she would be."

Barbara winced as she watched Steve's face fall. "That's all right," he said. "Get on down there. I'll see you tomorrow."

"Steve?" Barbara said plaintively.

"Oh, go on!" Steve snapped.

Sniffing back tears of hurt, Barbara scurried out of the house and slammed the door behind her. And they had been so glad to see one another! Why were they angry again?

* * *

"Is Dr. Weimer still seeing patients?" Steve asked as Sylvia preened like a little peacock.

"I'm not sure," Sylvia replied, unconsciously arching her back. "Would you care to sit down and talk to me until she is finished?"

Grinning, Barbara stuck her head around the door and winked at Steve. "Dr. Weimer is not only finished with her patients, she is through with her calls and doesn't have the beeper tonight." She took Steve's arm and quickly led him from the office, leaving Sylvia standing crestfallen in the middle of the floor. Once they were out of earshot, Barbara started to giggle. "I thought I better get you away from the office piranha before she got you for her collection."

"Aw, and I was looking forward to it!" Steve said in mock disappointment. Barbara laughed nervously. Ever since she and Steve had parted last night, she had been tense and anxious. How would it be between them tonight?

Steve's arm tightened around Barbara. "Let's go to your place," he said softly. Barbara nodded, anxious to come together with Steve, eager to use their physical rapport to reestablish their emotional closeness. They drove to her house in separate cars, meeting in a passionate frenzy at her door and moving as one into Barbara's bedroom.

They shed their clothes quickly, Steve for once as careless of his garments as Barbara. She reached out and drew Steve to her, feeling the passion mount inside of her. Roughly, harshly, Steve kissed her, drawing an equally forceful response from her. In the heat of their passion he drew Barbara down on the bed, stroking her breasts and caressing her soft thighs until she thought she would explode, then taking her wildly, frantically. Barbara responded with a ferocity to match his own, drawing her nails tantalizingly down Steve's shoulders and massaging his buttocks, drawing him closer to her. When the moment of complete

162

fulfillment was reached, they both shuddered in passionate ecstasy.

Afterward, Barbara lay beside Steve in the still silence. She was confused and dismayed. Physically they had pleasured each other as they always had, but on a deeper plane something was missing. That deep emotional bonding that had so characterized their unions had been absent tonight. Earlier in the day she could not wait to go to bed with Steve, so that they could smooth over the tensions between them, reestablish the close emotional rapport that they seemed to have lost. But it hadn't worked. They were just as far apart as they had been when they went to bed. Slowly she turned to Steve, to see him staring at the ceiling, frustration written all over his face. So it isn't just me, she thought. He felt it, too. She reached out and touched Steve's chest softly. "Steve?" she asked.

"Let's get some clothes on, Barbara," he said tiredly. "I think we need to talk." He rolled out of bed and reached for his underwear.

Sick with dread, Barbara hastily pulled on a pair of jeans and a top. She followed Steve into the kitchen, where he was making a pot of coffee. Silently they waited for the coffee to perk, not touching, not speaking. Barbara shivered a little from the fear that had turned her stomach into knots. How would he react to tonight's fiasco? Had it bothered him as much as it had bothered her?

Steve poured a steaming cup of coffee and handed it to Barbara. He poured another one for himself and followed her out to the living room. Sitting down, they faced one another as the atmosphere between them became charged. Steve swallowed a sip of coffee and sighed gently. "What happened tonight?" he asked finally.

"I'm not sure," Barbara admitted. "Physically it was all right, but . . ." She trailed off uncertainly.

"But it was empty," Steve said flatly. "Like it used to be for Shelley and me after we stopped getting along."

163

"Yeah," Barbara replied, stung that he had compared her to his ex-wife but knowing what he meant. "That happened to Wayne and me, too."

"And now it's happened to us," Steve said quietly. "Barbara, what are we going to do?"

"I don't know," she replied, running her fingers through her hair in agitation. "Oh, we never see each other anymore. You're too busy."

"You're damn right I'm busy," Steve replied. "I spent so much time courting you back in the fall I got behind. I have to get my work done sometime."

"Please, Steve, let's don't fight," Barbara pleaded. "We're both too busy. I always was, and now you are, too. Our time together is very limited. I guess we just have to live with that."

"We're not doing such a good job of living with it," Steve replied wryly. "This affair just isn't working, and we both know it."

"We haven't given it enough time!" Barbara replied quickly.

"Maybe not," Steve said. "But it still isn't what you thought it would be, is it?"

"No, it isn't," Barbara admitted. "So what can we do about it?"

Steve bit his lip. "I think we ought to get married."

"No," Barbara replied firmly, her insides tightening. Why did he have to bring that up again?

"Yes," Steve replied. "Or at least live together. I know I made a bad mistake the night Phil Harris died, but I honestly think I've learned my lesson. And if we were married or living together, we would have a lot more opportunity to see each other. Take last night. You had to go deliver a baby. Fine. But if we were together, you would have come home to me, and I could have slept with you in my arms, no matter how late it was. Instead you went home to your own place."

"But we're together tonight!" Barbara protested.

"And how many nights will go by before we can be together

164

again? Two? Three? A week? At least if we were married or living together, what little time we do have could be shared naturally. As it is, we're just another appointment on each other's calendar."

"Steve!" Barbara cried, horrified.

"It's true, Barbara. We'd do better to marry."

"I just can't, Steve, and you know why."

"Yes, I know why," Steve replied bitterly. "Because I blew it. One time, by God, I fell off the pedestal you put me on and you won't give me a chance with you." Steve stood up and grabbed his coat. "Good night, Barbara."

"Steve, wait!" she called as he walked toward the door. Barbara watched the front door close behind him, then she sat with a pillow cradled in her arms and stared out at the Houston lights. She was confused. Much of what Steve had said made sense. She had been willing to marry him before the night of Phil's death. But after the way he acted that night, could she believe him when he said that he would understand in the future? Did she dare take that chance? "Oh, God, I just can't!" Barbara moaned. "I just couldn't take it if it went wrong a second time."

Barbara sat at the mirror in her bathroom and listlessly pulled her brush through her hair. Steve had called earlier and asked if he could come by for a few minutes, and reluctantly Barbara had agreed to see him. What she had really wanted to do was crawl into her bed and pull the covers over her head for a week. But she wouldn't do that. Nor would she postpone the inevitable. He's coming over to break it off, Barbara said to herself, pulling her hair into a loose ponytail. And I really don't blame him. I'd break it off, too.

It went to pieces on me, Barbara thought as she pulled on her loafers, just like my marriage. Even I could see it this time. Since that bitter discussion in her living room almost six weeks earlier, Barbara had watched her relationship with Steve disintegrate right before her eyes. Oh, they had tried. They had seen each other as often as they could manage, and they even managed to have a few good times, but those became fewer and fewer as the relationship crumbled under the strain. They had made love on several occasions, but the emptiness was still there. Oh, they found physical release, all right, but that was the extent of their rapport. And that's just not enough, Barbara cried silently. That isn't enough for either one of us. Steve was plainly unhappy and didn't bother to hide it. And, much to her amazement, Barbara found herself bitterly dissatisfied with the relationship and not sure what had gone wrong. She had gotten her way, hadn't she? She had her affair. So why was she as unhappy as Steve?

Christmas had come and gone, with Barbara spending hers at the hospital and Steve with Scooter. Gradually, as the new year began, Steve called her less and less, finally stopping altogether. And tonight he's coming to do the gentlemanly thing and break it off formally, Barbara thought as pain tore through her heart.

Barbara answered the pealing doorbell and motioned for Steve to come in. He slipped out of his coat and sat down in the chair. Barbara sat down on the sofa and faced him with tears in her eyes. "Did you come to say good-bye?" she asked sadly.

"If I ask you to marry me again, will the answer still be no?" Steve said gravely.

"Yes, Steve, yes, it would," Barbara replied regretfully. "You know that I could never be the kind of wife that you need. There would be times that my being a doctor would have to come first."

"Then, yes, Barbara, I'm breaking it off," Steve said heart-brokenly.

"Oh, please, no!" Barbara cried involuntarily, anguish on her face. "I can be your lover!"

"Barbara, we've tried that, and it hasn't worked," Steve replied, his voice filled with pain. "It might have if I didn't love you so much. But I do, and I want to be with you. If it had been purely a sexual relationship, it might have been all right. But, damn it, we fell in love, and a damned affair just isn't enough for me."

"If we married, it wouldn't be any better," Barbara said softly. "We would still be busy."

"But what time we did have we could spend together," Steve replied. He jumped up from his chair and paced the floor in agitation. "Oh, hell, Barbara. Don't you understand? I know medicine has to come first a lot of the time with you, and I respect that. But don't you see? If you married me, then I would feel like I came first with you at least some of the time. This way it's second place for Steve all the way down the line. By refusing to marry me, you're refusing to give me any priority in your life. And that's what I can't stand. I would always be second place. I couldn't take that."

"But, Steve," Barbara said as tears started to run down her cheeks, "even if I did marry you I couldn't put you first. Why do you think I've fought you so hard? A husband deserves better."

"Then, I guess it's time to go," Steve replied quietly. He drew Barbara up out of the chair and took her into his arms. Slowly his mouth reached down and captured hers, drawing deeply from her depths. Barbara melted into him, knowing that this would be the last time these strong arms would hold her this way, and poured all the love she could into her embrace. Oh, she wanted to hold him forever, to scream that she would marry, do whatever he wanted, only please, don't go! But she couldn't. It wouldn't be fair to Steve. Clinging mindlessly to him, she willed this moment to last forever, the moment before he would walk out of her life for good.

The moment had to end. Slowly Steve pulled out of their embrace. He looked at Barbara's face one last time, as though memorizing her beloved features, then turned to the door, bright tears glistening in his eyes. "Good-bye, Barbara," he said softly.

Barbara watched the door close, then ran down the hall to her bedroom. Choking on sobs, she cursed the fates for ever having let her love Steve and for having to let him go. Sniffing, Barbara reached for a tissue and blew her nose hastily as the telephone rang. It was her exchange. She took down the number and went to the bathroom for a drink of water. Gulping down the cool liquid, she cleared her throat and dialed the number she had been given. "Sally? Dr. Weimer here. What seems to be the problem?"

CHAPTER TEN

How much longer is this afternoon going to go on? Barbara thought wearily as she trudged back and forth from one examining room to another. It was almost six, but a major flu epidemic had hit Houston about a week ago, and every family-practice specialist and pediatrician in town had been inundated with feverish, aching patients. Barbara hated flu epidemics, for although the vast majority of the victims would make a speedy recovery, there was always the chance that an older patient or an infant would become seriously ill or die. And then there was really very little she could do for those whom she treated. Since the flu was viral, there was no way she could combat it chemically. She had to rely on support therapy while the body battled the disease on its own. Tiredly she peeked out into the waiting room. Thank God there are only a few left, she thought, and some of them are Max's. As she walked past the kitchen, she noticed that Steve's skyscraper was almost finished. The open floor that she had walked out on was now enclosed by concrete, and the outdoor elevator was long gone.

Oh, Steve, why did it have to end the way it did? she thought before she could stop herself. Why couldn't it have worked for us? Quickly Barbara dragged her mind away from Steve. Don't let yourself think about it here, she chided herself immediately. You have patients who deserve your full attention. You can think about him and cry some more when you get home.

Actually, Barbara had cried very little since the first week that Steve had been gone. She had sobbed into her pillow every night for a week, then lethargy had taken over. Outwardly her behavior was the same as it always had been, but there was a hollow-

169

ness in her heart that all the sick patients in the world could not fill. She missed Steve. She missed him desperately! But there was nothing she could do about it.

Shutting the blinds in the kitchen, Barbara walked back out into the corridor and ran right into Eileen Vaughan, who was striding up the corridor at a furious pace. "Where's Max?" she demanded. "I have to talk to him, right now!" The tiny brunette was trembling with rage.

"He's with a patient," Barbara said shortly. She did not like Eileen Vaughan very much, and she did not bother to hide it. "You can wait for him in his office, or you can go home and call him later."

Eileen's jaw dropped. "I'll wait," she said stiffly as she swept into Max's office.

Barbara picked up the chart on Janet Barclay's baby and went into the examining room, immediately forgetting about Eileen. She had finished examining the squirming infant and was passing a pleasant moment chatting with Janet when Sylvia stuck her head in the door. "Dr. Weimer, what can I do?" she whispered frantically. "Marcie Brennan's here."

"So what?" Barbara asked. "Marcie's always coming to see Max."

"I know," Sylvia replied, agitated. "But Marcie wants to wait in Max's office and Eileen's already there."

"Oh, boy," Barbara whispered under her breath. "Stall Marcie for a minute until I get there." Barbara bade Janet and her baby good-bye and headed for the waiting room. Maybe if she offered Marcie the use of her own office, they could avoid Eileen and Marcie's coming face to face. Not that that wouldn't be funny, Barbara thought, on any other day. But today I can do without that.

Marcie Brennan, a large, buxom redhead, was pacing up and down in the waiting room, powdered and perfumed and ready for a night on the town. Barbara would have liked Marcie but for the demanding attitude with which she treated poor Max.

Breaking off her trot, she greeted Barbara warmly. "It's so good to see you again, Dr. Weimer," Marcie said. "Is Max almost ready to go? We have tickets to the opera, and I thought we could grab a bite to eat before we went."

"I don't know," Barbara stammered. Even if Max were through, Eileen would be sure to tie him up for at least half an hour.

"Well, then, I'd like to wait in his office, if you don't mind," Marcie said nonchalantly, striding confidently for the door.

Oh, help! Barbara thought. "Uh, Marcie, would you like to wait in my office? Max is probably making phone calls right now."

"I don't mind." Marcie laughed.

"You can't go into his office!" Sylvia blurted suddenly. "Eileen's in there."

Sylvia, your mouth is as big as your bustline, Barbara thought disgustedly. Marcie's face took on a positively menacing smile. "Why, Eileen is just the person I'd most like to visit with for a few moments," she purred silkily as she marched past Barbara and pushed open Max's door. "Hello, Eileen," she said deliberately. "I'm Marcella Brennan."

"You're the bitch who put him up to it!" Eileen spat as she stood up. Even in heels she was a good six inches shorter than Marcie, and she had a temper like a firecracker. Barbara followed Marcie to Max's office, apprehension warring with amusement. Whatever happened to poor Max in the next few minutes, this was going to be good! "Max was supposed to take the kids tonight, but you got him to cancel! That isn't fair!" Eileen snapped. "My evening has been planned for weeks. Max," she wailed as her unsuspecting ex-husband walked into the room, "you can't let me down at this late date! You said you'd take the kids!"

"I—uh . . ." Max started to stutter.

"Why don't you hire a baby-sitter?" Marcie asked condescendingly. She strode up to Max and slid her arms around his

171

neck. "Explain to Eileen that you have already made plans to go out with me."

"Well, I—uh . . ." Max repeated.

"But you told me *weeks* ago that you would take the kids out tonight," Eileen snapped. "And then she talked you into abandoning them! Your own children! You ought to be ashamed!"

"Ashamed! That's a laugh," Marcie sneered patronizingly. "All you want is an unpaid baby-sitter. You ought to grow up. Max," she said warningly, "we're going to be late." Barbara noticed that Max's face was getting very red.

"You would rather spend the evening with that home-wrecker than with your own children. Some father you are!" Eileen sneered.

"Home-wrecker! Why, you spoiled brat . . ."

"*Enough!*" Max roared at the top of his lungs. Both women broke off their wrangling and stared at him in horror. "First off, Eileen, I did not promise to keep the kids tonight. I said I might, if it was convenient. It is not. Therefore, take your plaintive wails and your accusations and *get the hell out of here!*"

Once again Eileen's jaw dropped. "Why, you can't talk to me like that!"

"I just did." Max grinned. "And if you're not out of here in two seconds flat I'm going to do it again." Red faced, Eileen marched out of the office and left the building, slamming the door behind her.

Marcie glided toward Max and slid her arm through his. "It's getting late, darling. We'd better go." She reached into her purse, pulled out the tickets, and handed them to Max.

Calmly Max tore the tickets in half. "I hate the opera," he said calmly. "I especially hate it when a pushy broad is dragging me against my will. The next time I want to go on a date, I'll call you."

Marcie's face turned a bright shade of red. "Don't bother to call, Max," she said haughtily. "I'll be busy." She held her head high and left his office regally.

Barbara ran to her office and slammed the door. She bent over her desk and howled with laughter. She knew that Max and Sylvia could hear her, but she couldn't help it. Max had finally put those two in their place, and he had done it so well.

As Barbara was dialing the last number on her list, Max poked his head in the door. "As you might have guessed, I'm without female companionship this evening. Care to eat with me?" He sneezed and grinned outrageously at Barbara.

"I-I guess so," Barbara stammered. She hadn't had an evening out in weeks, and she needed one, but she was afraid that she wouldn't be very good company tonight. Still, she hated to tell Max no. She made the last of her calls and met Max in the hall. "Where to?" she asked lightly.

"Lucy's?" Max asked casually.

Oh, no, she couldn't go there! Not with all the memories that place held. "No, Max, not Lucy's," Barbara said quickly. "How about that new burger bar near the hospital?"

Puzzled, Max nodded. "Meet you there," he said as they walked out the door.

Thirty minutes later Max and Barbara were seated in a cozy booth in the small, crowded hamburger bar. Barbara had ordered a simple burger, and Max had requested the house special, a chili burger with fried onions. "I hope you're not planning to kiss anybody after an order like that!" Barbara teased.

"Who would I kiss?" Max laughed, coughing a little. "I hate to admit it, but it sure felt good to get those two off my back for a while."

"Do you suppose Marcie meant it when she said she wouldn't be back?" Barbara asked.

"Sure she did," Max replied unconcernedly. "And frankly, my dear, I don't give a damn."

"I think I've heard that line somewhere before," Barbara said dryly. "Oh, well, with your looks you won't have any trouble replacing her."

"I'm not sure I want to," Max said honestly. "And talking about replacements, what happened to Steve Sullivan? Sylvia and I were sure he was going to be husband number two."

Barbara's hands started to shake and she dropped the napkin she had been holding. "We broke up over a month ago," she admitted quietly. "It wasn't working out."

"That's a shame," Max said frankly. "He was a nice guy."

"Yes, he was," Barbara mumbled, tears springing to her eyes. Of all people, she did not want to talk about Steve tonight.

But Max blithely pursued the discussion, not realizing the pain he was causing Barbara. "Yes, Sylvia and I had laid bets that you two would be married by spring. It was really hot and heavy there for a while, wasn't it?"

"Max, damn it, do you mind?" Barbara snapped as she brushed tears from her eyes. "I'd rather not talk about it."

"Oops, big-mouthed Max has done it again," he replied ruefully. "Sorry, Barbara. I didn't mean to hurt you."

"That's all right," Barbara replied, trying to keep her voice steady. "You didn't know how badly it hurt me."

"Barbara, would you like to tell me about it?" Max asked gently as the waitress put their plates in front of them. "Maybe I can help."

Barbara sighed. She really didn't want to talk about Steve, but maybe if she could get her feelings out in the open, some of the pain would go away. So she nodded and picked up her hamburger, nibbling at the bun. Now that she had ordered the burger, she didn't think she'd be able to finish it. "Eat up," Max ordered her. "And then we'll talk."

Barbara gagged down about a third of the hamburger, finally pushing the plate away when she realized that it was hopeless. Max finished his meal with relish and ordered them both another beer. Gratefully Barbara swallowed the cold brew, thankful that she could at least manage that. As the waitress picked up their plates, Max reached into his pocket and pulled out his pipe.

"Okay, tell Uncle Max what happened," he said, putting a match to the bowl.

"It's a long story," Barbara replied hesitantly. "But basically it boils down to the fact that Steve wants to get married and I can't. So we tried an affair, but that didn't work, either. So we broke up."

"Well, you did boil it down, all right," Max said dryly. "He wants marriage, and you say you can't. Why can't you?"

"Max, don't you remember what happened to my last marriage?" Barbara asked. "It broke up because I was a rotten wife. I can't inflict that on another man."

"So what went wrong with the affair?" Max asked quietly, puffing slowly on the pipe.

"We never could be together enough," Barbara replied sadly. "One of us was always busy. The relationship withered away."

"How did Steve feel about you?" Max asked quietly.

A shaft of pain tore through Barbara. "He loved me," she choked. "He loved me a lot."

"Then, why did you let him go?" Max asked incredulously.

"Oh, Max, I couldn't be a decent wife to him!" Barbara cried in anguish. "Look what happened with Wayne. I tried for six years to do right by him, and I just couldn't. It wouldn't be any different with anybody else."

"Of course you couldn't be a good wife to Wayne. The man was a selfish bastard," Max said dryly.

"No, he wasn't," Barbara protested in shock.

"Yes, he was," Max repeated. "He resented your career like hell, because he wasn't smart enough to be a doctor himself. He did everything he could to make it hard on you. I don't think you ever realized that."

"No, I didn't," Barbara replied, astonished. She hadn't realized that Max felt that way about Wayne.

Max stopped for a moment and puffed on his pipe. "Was Steve Sullivan like that?"

"Yes—no—I don't know," Barbara admitted bewilderedly.

"Sometimes he was just great, like the time he brought me the pie." At Max's puzzled look, she told him about the night Mrs. Valdez had died. "But the night I was trying to save Phil Harris, he was just horrid. I missed a party he was giving and he was furious."

"How did he act when he found out what had happened?" Max asked quietly, coughing into his napkin.

"He was very sorry he had yelled at me," Barbara admitted, running her fingers through her hair. "And he never acted put out again when I was called away."

"And you're going to write the poor man off for one slip?" Max asked reprovingly.

"That's not why I won't marry him!" Barbara snapped, irate. "It isn't fair to Steve. He deserves to come first in his wife's life, at least some of the time, and I could never give him first place."

"Why not?" Max challenged her quietly. "At least some of the time."

"But the practice . . ."

Max uttered a very rude word about the practice. "Look, you have every other weekend free, and lots of evenings you aren't tied up. Do you think your situation is so different from that of a young businesswoman or any other professional woman who wants to get ahead? Lots of them manage a husband and a career. Sure, medicine takes a lot of your time, but it doesn't take all of it. Why couldn't your husband have those precious moments when you are free?"

"I just don't know, though," Barbara protested, wanting to agree with Max but afraid. She ran her fingers through her hair in agitation. "How would we ever work out a marriage, if we couldn't even manage an affair?"

"Of course you couldn't manage an affair," Max said as he reached into his pocket for a handkerchief. He blew his nose and continued. "You aren't the type of woman to be content with an affair, if you loved the man. Oh, Barbara, you deserve so much more than an affair," he added as he stuffed the handkerchief back into his pocket. "Yes, it would be a delicate balance between your career and your marriage. Steve would have to be patient and understanding when you were busy, and you would have to be careful to plan times when you didn't have the beeper to be with him and to do things with him. But if what you say about him is true, he must want very much to make a marriage work with you, and I'll bet an office full of OB patients that he would work just as hard at maintaining that balance as you would."

"Do you really think so?" Barbara asked doubtfully.

"Yes, I do," Max said as he picked up the check. "Who knows, I may achieve a delicate balance someday myself. But I mean it, Barbara," he added seriously. "Think about it."

"I will," Barbara promised.

"Dr. Weimer, I'm sorry," Sylvia apologized as Barbara peered out wearily at the packed office. It was nearly six and there were at least seven more patients who had to be seen, plus a good two hours' worth of telephone calls to make. "They're all really sick and I could hardly turn them away," Sylvia added.

"That's all right," Barbara replied tiredly as she tied a piece of string around her hair. Max sure picked a great time to get the flu, she thought as she picked up the next chart and headed for the examining room. Max had called her with a high fever and severe chills the morning after they had eaten supper together. Barbara had gone over to his apartment and confirmed what Max had already told her. He had a bad case of the flu that was going around. Barbara had ordered him the same treatment that all her flu patients got—plenty of rest and aspirin for the aches and fever. She'd then called the hospital and arranged for one of the senior residents in family practice to see patients for a few hours in the mornings until Max was well, but Barbara was still left with the work of almost two practices on her shoulders. Most evenings she was not getting out of the office until eight or eight thirty, and she had the beeper for both her patients and Max's.

177

Her hectic schedule had left her almost no time to do anything besides work, although during the occasional moment alone she would think about Max's belief that she and Steve could have made a go of a marriage. I just don't know, she thought. I'm just not convinced. But when Max gets back and I don't have so much to do, I'll sit down and really think it over.

Barbara glanced down at the chart she was holding as she strode into the examining room, and Margo Langly's name jumped out at her. Trying to hide her shock and the painful associations that Margo held for her, Barbara walked into the room. A much thinner Margo was sitting on the examining table, coughing. She looked up and greeted Barbara with a thin smile. "How are you, Dr. Weimer?" she asked.

"Do you want an honest answer?" Barbara replied wryly.

"Let me guess. Dr. Vaughan ran off with the secretary and . . ." Both women laughed.

"No, he has the flu, just like you seem to," Barbara said as she picked up a stethoscope and listened to Margo's chest. She examined Margo thoroughly. "Yes, it's definitely the flu," Barbara said. "You need to stay at home for the next few days and take aspirin for the discomfort." She made a note in Margo's chart. "And you need to discontinue the diet pills until you're well."

"I don't take them anymore," Margo admitted sheepishly. "I only took them a week. They made me hang off the ceiling."

"Really?" Barbara replied, surprised and not bothering to hide it. Margo had lost at least twenty-five pounds. "Then, how did you take off the weight?"

"Starvation," Margo admitted wryly. "Lots of green salad."

"Well, you look great, except for the flu," Barbara told her warmly.

"How about you?" Margo asked. "How are you doing with Max out?"

"Frankly, I'm running ragged," Barbara admitted. "But I've always thrived on work, so I'll be all right. Now, remember, don't go back to work until you're completely recovered."

"Steve's gonna love me," Margo said dryly, unwittingly cutting Barbara to the quick. "Be seeing you later, Dr. Weimer."

Oh, why, oh, why had Margo said that about Steve? Barbara agonized as she drove home in the late-February chill. Although Margo's comment had been made in jest, the thought of Steve loving another woman had torn Barbara's insides to pieces. Why did she have to remind me of Steve? I didn't want to think about him tonight. I wanted to rest. But you have to think about him, she reminded herself. You have to think about him, and what he means to you, and you have to decide whether you're willing to take a chance on marrying him.

Impulsively Barbara turned on the blinker and steered her car onto the expressway, even though it was not the closest way to get home. She had to think, and the expressway at this time of night was not so crowded as to make total concentration on her driving necessary. Besides, it would provide her with a brief respite from the beeper. As she drove, she went over her conversation with Max sentence by sentence. He thought she and Steve could have made a go of it. He knew Steve and he had known Wayne, and he honestly thought that Steve and Barbara could have made a marriage work.

She drove past the exit to the hospital, remembering the times that Steve had sat in the doctors' lounge willingly waiting for her to finish with a patient. She took a cloverleaf and drove past the exit to Lucy's, and a slight smile played around her lips when she remembered that piece of pie that Steve had arranged for her to eat on the way to the hospital. She drove past the Galleria, huge and brightly lit, and she remembered skating with Steve on the ice and the way she had laughed at him when he fell down. A thin coating of tears filmed her eyes. If she stayed on this leg of the expressway, in just a few blocks it would connect with the highway that would take her to the coast. She sniffed back tears, remembering the passion-filled weekend they had spent there.

Barbara brushed the tears from her eyes and took the next

exit, turning under the expressway and getting back on it in the opposite direction. Speeding a little, she drove to her own exit and drove down the dimly lighted streets to her condominium. Barbara parked in her carport and fished around in her purse for a key. She would make herself a sandwich and go on to bed, hoping that she did not get a midnight call from the exchange. Walking slowly to her front door, she jumped and screamed softly when the huge shadow of a man fell across her path.

"Barbara, don't scream!" a familiar voice said softly.

"Steve?" Barbara asked without turning around. It was her imagination. It had to be. Steve had left her weeks ago. It was somebody else who sounded like him.

"Barbara, it really is me," Steve's voice said softly. Still unbelieving, Barbara turned around slowly, trembling like a leaf. In the dim light she could not see him clearly, but she knew it was Steve. Slowly she extended her hand and touched the familiar scar above his left eyebrow.

"I thought it was my imagination," Barbara breathed quietly.

"Let's go in the house. It's freezing out here," Steve said as he took Barbara's arm and led her to the front door. With trembling fingers she unlocked the door and let Steve in first. He immediately headed for the kitchen. *What is he doing here?* Barbara wondered. *We broke it off for good.* She began to tremble, sick with love and longing for him. *Doesn't he realize how much it hurts me to see him, even now?*

Masking her emotions as best she could, Barbara followed Steve into the kitchen. He was standing at the sink, his back to her, unloading a sack of groceries. "Margo said you were taking care of both practices," Steve volunteered. "I figured you were living on sandwiches and thought you needed a decent meal."

"Th-thanks," Barbara stammered. *Margo must have told him about Max when she called in sick. But why had he come over? Their relationship was finished. Was he just being generous? I don't want you to be generous,* Barbara thought stubbornly, but she did not say it out loud.

She watched silently as Steve unwrapped two juicy club steaks and put them on the broiler. "You have time for a shower before supper if you hurry," Steve volunteered as he turned around from the sink. Looking at him, Barbara gasped in horror. Always lean, he had dropped somewhere between ten and fifteen pounds since she had seen him last, and the hollows in his cheeks and the circles under his eyes gave him a positively haggard look. "Steve, you look terrible!" she exclaimed.

"You don't look much better," he replied acidly as he returned to the meal.

In her bathroom Barbara stripped off her clothes and showered quickly. Stepping out of the shower, she toweled herself dry and stared at herself in the mirror. No, she had not lost any weight, but the usual circles under her eyes had darkened almost to black, and her skin was pasty. Her face wore a pinched, sad expression that showed even when she smiled. "He's right," she said out loud. "I look about as bad as he does." She pulled on a pair of jeans and a T-shirt and wandered slowly back to the kitchen, watching Steve as he put the finishing touches on their meal. She looked like this because her schedule had been grueling, but why did Steve look so bad? She longed to ask him, but, afraid of another rebuff, she held her tongue and set the dining-room table.

"It's ready," Steve said as he carried their two plates into the dining room. In spite of her emotional torment Barbara was starving, and she ate every bite of her steak. Steve was only picking at his, she noticed ruefully. She got up from the table, returning with a bottle of wine and two wineglasses, and poured Steve a glass.

"This will help stimulate your appetite," she said quietly.

Steve tossed back the entire glass in one gulp. Grimacing, Barbara poured herself a glass and sat back down. "Thank you for supper," she said, wondering again why he had come over this evening. "It's the first decent meal I've had in three days."

"I'm glad you enjoyed it," Steve said dully. He poured himself

181

another glass of wine and drank it, but did not eat any more of his steak.

"Why have you lost so much weight?" Barbara blurted, the pain of seeing him like this overruling good manners.

"Overwork. Not enough sleep. Not enough to eat," Steve admitted.

"You're killing yourself," Barbara said sternly. "I thought you were the one who led the balanced life."

"I did," Steve replied. "Until you came in and tipped over the balance."

I did that? Barbara asked herself, stunned.

He got up and marched his plate to the kitchen, then reached into his pocket and took out a pack of cigarettes. With trembling fingers he lit one and inhaled deeply.

"You don't smoke," Barbara said accusingly. "When did you start that?" She cringed, knowing exactly what that cigarette was doing to Steve's lungs.

"I started up again about a month ago," Steve replied, taking another puff.

Right after we broke up, Barbara thought. My God! The weight loss, the overwork, the cigarettes! Had losing her done this to him? Reaching out slowly, she touched Steve's arm, flinching when he pulled away from her.

Suddenly she had to know. "Steve, why did you come back?" she asked gently.

Steve turned away from her. Barbara held her breath. "Steve?" she said quietly.

"I came because I couldn't stay away," he said as he turned to her, anguish in his face.

"Oh, Steve!" she sobbed, launching herself across the room at him. His arms opened wide and he held her in a huge, warm embrace, loving and welcoming. "I've missed you so much!" she said over and over into Steve's shirtfront.

"God, I've missed you, Barbara," Steve said quietly as he pressed her head onto his shoulder. He clung to her desperately.

as a drowning man might cling to a life raft, afraid to let go of the one thing that meant all to him.

Barbara lifted her head and looked into Steve's eyes, her own burning with unfulfilled need. "I need you so badly, Steve. I need you the way I have never needed anything or anyone ever before." She shook in his arms with love and longing.

"Do you mean that, Barbara? Do you really mean that?" Steve begged her urgently.

Barbara nodded. Steve swept her off her feet and carried her to the bedroom, where Barbara pushed two loads of clothes off the bed onto the floor. He reached out and turned off the overhead light, leaving the room bathed in the soft glow of a single table lamp, then reached out and touched Barbara gently on the arm. "Are you sure you want to do this?" he asked softly.

Without answering him, she slowly pulled off the T-shirt, her naked breasts glowing whitely in the dim light of the little lamp. As Steve watched, she boldly removed her jeans and her panties and stood before him naked and unashamed. "I want to make love to you, Steve," she murmured quietly. "I need to."

Groaning in surrender, Steve pulled her to him and folded her into his arms, drawing her close to every inch of his body. The rough material of his shirt scraped Barbara's sensitive breasts and his belt buckle poked her in the waist, but she did not care. It had been so long since she and Steve had really made love, and she needed him so badly. "Oh, Steve," she whispered as his mouth captured hers.

It began as a gentle kiss, but as the passion began to flow between them, Steve's mouth became hard and demanding, drawing Barbara into his passionate vortex. She responded instantly, explosively, reaching up and wrapping her arms around him and pulling him closer to her. Steve ran his fingers down Barbara's back and sides, raising shivers of pleasure everywhere his hands roamed. She reached down and, without breaking the sensual contact of their mouths, began to unbutton his shirt. She

183

got as far as the third button but could go no farther since their bodies were tightly entwined from that point on.

Reluctantly Steve removed his mouth from hers. "I guess I'd better help you," he whispered. Quickly he finished unbuttoning his shirt and dropped it to the floor, and his pants and briefs soon followed. Now as naked as she, he reached out and drew Barbara to him, slowly pushing her down on the bed. "I never thought I would touch you like this again," he whispered as he stroked her body lovingly.

"Oh, God, Steve, I've missed you so much," Barbara whispered back, remembering all the nights she had spent dreaming of Steve, longing for him. She reached out and touched his warm chest tentatively; then, as her fingers grew bolder, she touched his nipples, grazing them with her mouth. "I can't believe it's really you. You came back."

"God, yes, I came back," Steve replied, anguish in his voice, his arms tightening around her. "I missed you so badly. I would wake up in the middle of the night and reach for you, but you weren't there. I would reach for the phone to call you, but then I'd remember that we weren't seeing each other anymore, and I'd want to scream. I'd—"

"Hush, Steve," Barbara said gently. "I'm here, and you can hold me and make love to me and whatever I can do to make you happy again, I'll do it." She wanted to love him, to give to him, to make up for all the pain she had caused this wonderful man. Suddenly the act of love took on a new meaning for Barbara, as her love for Steve placed this physical act in a new emotional dimension. Wanting desperately to love him fully, she reached out and caressed his bare waist with her warm fingers, moving enticingly down his hips, causing him to shudder as his thighs pressed against hers. She drew his waiting body to her.

Steve dipped his head and kissed her breast softly, tickling one nipple with his tongue until it was swollen and hard on his lips. Barbara reached out and feverishly stroked his shoulders and his back, loving him with her tender touch. She reached out with her foot and ran it up and down Steve's legs, loving the feel of the hair-roughened legs tangling with her own smooth ones. Steve trailed his mouth across to her other breast, and he caressed it gently with his mouth until it, too, was hard. "Oh, Steve," Barbara murmured, "I've missed that so."

"Have you missed this?" Steve asked softly, allowing his hand to drift lower until it was rubbing her flat stomach in a teasing circular pattern.

"Yes!" Barbara murmured as her stomach muscles contracted in rhythm with his fingers. His fingers strayed even lower, and Barbara cried out in longing. "I've missed the way you touch me, the way you hold me, the way you make me feel like the most special woman in the world," she whispered.

He covered every inch of her face with loving kisses. Barbara moaned in delight as his hands and lips caressed every inch of her warm, loving body. Her own hands roamed freely over his shoulders, his sides, his firm rounded buttocks, touching and teasing and tormenting him until he was out of his mind with pleasure. With all the love that she had for him, Barbara touched Steve's body gently, tenderly, drawing his hips closer to hers in sensual intimacy. Steve wrapped his arms around her and let her feel his powerful need for her, then he gently nudged her legs open with his and became one with her again.

Open and vulnerable as they had never been with one another before, Barbara and Steve made love with hungry desperation, pouring all the love and the hurt and the longing that they felt for each other into their embrace. Murmuring sweet words, they moved together, holding back nothing. Their lovemaking held all the passion that it ever had, but now they also shared the loneliness, the uncertainty, the pain, that they had felt without each other. It was as though the joining of their bodies had also forced a forging of their souls, allowing each one to glimpse the torment of the other. Wildly, sadly, happily, passionately, they moved together in a building tempo, the flaming passion of their bodies searing their souls together. Profoundly moved, Barbara called out Steve's name at the moment of delight, whispering his name over and over as he joined her in that glorious place.

Spent, exhausted, they lay wrapped tightly together. Cradled in Steve's arms, her head on his chest, Barbara stared vacantly into space. I didn't realize, she thought over and over. I didn't know until now just how much he loves me. Not until he made love to me like that. Oh, Steve, I love you, she thought. I love you and I can't live without you.

Suddenly Barbara was aware that Steve's chest was shaking spasmodically. Slowly she raised her head and was horrified to see him trying to stifle sobs, tears running freely down his cheeks. She reached out to him and gripped his hand tightly in her own. "Don't cry, Steve, please don't cry."

Steve sat up in bed and pulled the covers up to his waist, never letting go of Barbara's hand. "We have to work something out, Barbara," he said firmly, valiantly ignoring his own tears. "I can't eat, I can't sleep, I work all hours of the day and night trying to forget you." He reached up and brushed the tears from his cheeks. "I knew if I came here tonight that I could never walk away from you again."

"I don't want you to," Barbara whispered, tears of her own running down her cheeks. She wiped her eyes on the sheet. "I've spent too many nights alone in this lonely bed. I want to work something out."

"You do?" Steve asked faintly.

Barbara nodded, sniffing. Steve reached out and gathered her to him, his thin body racked with sobs. "Oh, you're crying again," Barbara exclaimed.

"Only because I'm happy," Steve replied as he took a deep breath and willed himself to stop. He wiped his cheeks with a fistful of Barbara's hair and propped up the pillows, leaning back against them and pulling Barbara's head onto his shoulder. He took Barbara's hand and looked at it in surprise. "You still have on the coral ring," he said quietly.

"I couldn't bear to take it off," Barbara admitted. "It was all I had left of you."

"Oh, Barbara," Steve whispered gently. "You don't know how happy that makes me." They lay together, happy, yet knowing that they still had a lot of ground to cover.

Finally Steve spoke. "Do you want to go back to the affair?" he asked her quietly. "I guess if we tried harder, it would work." Steve's arm tightened around Barbara's waist.

"I don't think so," Barbara said frankly, running her fingers through the hair on his chest. "We tried that before, and it was miserable."

"Then, what do we do?" Steve asked quietly. "Marriage is out, and the affair didn't work. What else is there?"

"Steve, how did you achieve the balance in your life—the balance that you had before you met me?" Barbara asked softly.

"I worked at it," Steve said. "I set my priorities, I juggled my time, and I was selfish sometimes, I guess."

"Do you think we could manage something like that together?" Barbara asked hesitantly.

"What are you talking about?" Steve asked, confused.

Barbara pulled away from Steve and sat in front of him, so she could see his face. "I mean, do you think we could achieve a balance together? Max said we could."

"What does Max have to do with any of this?" Steve asked patiently.

"I spilled my guts to him the other night, and he said that he thought I could achieve a balance between my profession and you." Barbara twirled a strand of hair between her fingers. "You know, be a doctor and a good wife to you at the same time. He said that a lot of what happened before was Wayne's fault. I never realized that. I thought it was me."

"I figured all along that that might have been the case, but since I wasn't sure, I didn't say anything." He reached out and caressed Barbara's face gently. "I can't see how you could be a rotten wife to any man."

187

"But what about the times when you need me and I'm not there?" Barbara asked urgently. "Like the night Phil Harris died? I let you down that night, and I can't promise that it won't happen again."

Steve reached out and took Barbara's hand. "I let you down just as badly that night, and I can't promise that it won't happen again, either. I'm only human, and sometimes I'm sure I'll wish you were with me. But that works both ways, Barbara. Didn't you miss me the week I was in Mexico?"

"Oh, yes!" Barbara exclaimed.

"So we'll both miss one another sometimes. And I'll shop for your party clothes and run you to the hospital if your beeper goes off during the party. And you can buy me some more books to read while I wait for you to finish your work at the hospital. And we'll schedule anything important for the weekends you're off."

"And we'll go away a lot on my free weekends," Barbara said, picking up the thread of Steve's thought. "We could buy a condominium at the coast to escape to. I'll bring you and Margo hamburgers on my way to the hospital when you have to work late. And I'll learn to fix some quick easy meals for the nights when I get home first." She looked at Steve plaintively. "Will you really understand when I have to be gone? You won't resent me?"

"Never," Steve promised her firmly. "Just as you won't resent me when I have to be gone or out of town."

"I never thought of it like that," Barbara admitted. She frowned as another thought occurred to her. "What about children?" she asked hesitantly. "Most men want to have a child."

Steve smiled. "Barbara, I already have a child. Look, if you want one of our own later, I'd be willing, but if you don't, I sure don't expect it."

Barbara's mind was whirling. The future, full and bright, was unfolding in front of her. She looked at Steve with a sense of wonder. "We could do it, couldn't we? We could manage a balance, we could really do it!"

"It would be a delicate balance sometimes," Steve admitted. "And we'll have to be ready to forgive each other for not being perfect, but, yes, we could achieve that, Barbara. I'm sure of it."

"Oh, Steve," Barbara whispered. "I'm so happy!" He reached for her and she melted into his arms, glowing with happiness. Steve enfolded her to him and held her passionately, clinging to the woman who had just made his life complete again. "I'm sorry for the hell I put you through," she whispered softly. "I didn't know. I wish I had it to do over again."

"Maybe it's better this way," Steve replied solemnly as he held her tight. "This way we found out just how much we mean to each other." He pulled her to him and kissed her with love and longing, bearing her down onto the bed and covering her body with his own. So wrapped up were they with their lovemaking, they barely heard the telephone ring.

"I think your profession summons," Steve said against her lips.

"Hell," Barbara muttered as she sat up, brushing her hair out of her face.

"Don't get upset, Barbara," Steve said firmly. "It's all right. It really is." From the tender warmth in his eyes Barbara knew he was telling the truth. Grateful, she gave Steve a quick hug.

Barbara answered the telephone and took down the number. "It's Netta Morris," she said, grinning. "I won't have to go out, but I may be a while." She looked at Steve's too-thin body critically. "Go make a sandwich with the rest of your steak. You aren't such a hot advertisement for my competence as a doctor."

Steve sighed out loud. "We've been engaged all of ten minutes and you're already giving me orders." He ducked out the door as Barbara threw a pillow at him.

When Steve returned to the bedroom, clutching a fat sandwich in his hand, Barbara was sitting in the bed, propped up on the pillows, a huge grin on her face. "Didn't you call Netta?" Steve asked as he took a huge bite out of the sandwich.

"Yes," she said wickedly. Barbara laughed as Steve continued

189

to devour the sandwich. "She said I sounded funny and asked if I was in bed. I said yes, I was, and that I had just gotten engaged. She said congratulations, that she would call me in the morning, and then she hung up! Can you believe it?"

"Knowing you, I'd believe anything. But most of all, I believe I love you!" Steve exclaimed as he reached out and pulled Barbara into his arms. Barbara went to him willingly, joyously, knowing in her heart that the delicate balance would be forever theirs.

LOOK FOR NEXT MONTH'S
CANDLELIGHT ECSTASY ROMANCES ®